My name is Callum Ormond.
I am fifteen
and I am a hunted fugitive . . .

BOOK ONE: JANUARY

To Cassie Rose McDonald

First American Edition 2010
Kane Miller, A Division of EDC Publishing

Text copyright © Gabrielle Lord, 2009
Cover design copyright © Scholastic Australia, 2009
Illustrations copyright © Scholastic Australia, 2009
Back cover photo of boy's face © Scholastic Australia, 2009
Cover photo of boy © Scholastic Australia, 2009
Cover design by Natalie Winter
Illustrations by Rebecca Young
First published by Scholastic Australia Pty Limited in 2009
This edition published under licence from Scholastic Australia Pty Limited

For information contact:
Kane Miller, A Division of EDC Publishing
P.O. Box 470663
Tulsa, OK 74147-0663
www.kanemiller.com
www.edcpub.com

Library of Congress Control Number: 2009934732

Printed and bound in the United States of America
3 4 5 6 7 8 9 10
ISBN: 978-1-935279-49-5

CONSPIRACY 365

BOOK ONE: JANUARY

GABRIELLE LORD

Kane Miller
A DIVISION OF EDC PUBLISHING

Prologue

31 DECEMBER

New Year's Eve
Flood Street, Richmond

11:25 am

It was the wild, billowing black cloak, streaming behind the menacing figure, that first caught my eye. I was walking home from the park when the sight of it stopped me in my tracks. Something or someone was staggering up my street. *The grim reaper?*

I'd been out with Boges, kicking around a ball, and was heading back home to help pack the car for what Mum was calling "the usual family New Year's shenanigans" up the coast at Treachery Bay. Poor Boges was staying at home with his mum and his gran. They'd probably struggle to stay awake watching the nine o'clock fireworks on TV. My night was going to be tough, but at least we'd be away from it, out on the boat.

The commotion down the road came closer.

As the swooping shape neared, I saw that it was a muttering, gray-looking man. He was wearing a dark bathrobe and had a weird, lopsided run, as if he was off-balance and dizzy. I was just about to cross the road to avoid him when I made out what he was saying. With a rush of fear, I realized it was me he was coming after! "Cal!" he screamed. "Callum Ormond!"

He stumbled towards me, his wild eyes almost bursting from their sockets. He half-limped, half-ran, his flailing arms reaching out in front of him.

A siren wailed in the distance and within seconds an ambulance with flashing lights appeared at the other end of my street. It was driving towards us, fast.

The crazy man was almost on top of me. I could smell his foul, musty breath.

"Keep away from it, Callum!" he spluttered as drool fell from his gaping mouth. "They killed your father. They're killing me!"

My heart froze in my chest. Who was this guy? Did he mean the virus? The mention of my dad carried a wave of pain so huge, it sent my mind spinning. The man lunged at me.

"Who are you?!" I shouted, pushing him off. "What are you talking about?! How did you know my dad?"

The ambulance screeched to a halt next to us, and before the man could grab me again, two paramedics jumped out. The first tackled him while the second pulled something out of his bag. The madman on the ground clawed desperately at my feet.

"Who are you?" I shouted again. "Nobody killed my dad — he was sick!"

"Leave this to us, young man," said the first paramedic, who was gruff and built like a wrestler. "He doesn't know what he's talking about. You need to get out of the way."

Pinned down, the man was trapped, but as the second paramedic forced an injection into his wasted arm, he managed to twist towards me. His face was contorted, the veins in his neck pulsed and protruded.

He stared into my eyes. "The Ormond Singularity," he said, between gasps of breath. "Don't let it be the death of you too, boy! Get out! Get away! Hide and lay low until midnight December 31st of next year. You don't know what you're up against. Listen to me! Please! 365 days, Cal. You have 365 days!"

"Until what? What am I up against?" The demented man's menacing words had rocked me to my soul.

"What are you talking about?" I demanded.

"And what's the Ormond Singularity? How do you know who I am? Tell me who *you* are!"

The wrestler-medic sidled up beside me with a stretcher, and with a quick movement towards the man, he pushed me out of the way. "Our patient is very sick and his mind is affected. Please leave this to us and get on your way!"

With superhuman strength, the sick man tore himself away from the medics' hold. His eyes were wide with terror. "If you don't disappear, you're going to have to survive them for a whole year! Do you realize what that means? They're going to be after you for 365 days! Week after week! Day after day!"

My confusion and fear deepened. *Them?* Who was "them?" "What are you talking about?" I asked again. "*Who*'s after me?"

The sick man's sudden surge of strength collapsed. The medics quickly strapped him down on the stretcher. His head fell to one side and his eyelids blinked, furiously fighting the sedative taking over his bloodstream. His voice continued in a haunting and harsh whisper: "Callum, the Ormond Singularity. The others already know. They know your father contacted you. They will *kill* you. You must go into hiding until December 31st next year. Get your family to leave. Until midnight on the last day of the year . . . that's when the Singularity runs out. You're not safe until then. Somehow you must survive."

His eyes rolled back and his body fell limp. The paramedics carried him away.

"Don't pay any attention," called out the second medic. "Poor guy's been delusional for days. It's just getting worse. Don't let him worry you."

As the man was pushed into the back of the ambulance, he lifted his head one last time. "Cal," he moaned, "365 days. Once they . . . the angel . . . you must . . . for Tom . . ."

The doors slammed and the ambulance sped off.

In a few moments, silence closed in. I stood there alone and bewildered. It was like nothing had happened. The only sounds now were the distant barking of a dog, and the rustling of leaves in the trees that lined the street.

1 JANUARY

365 days to go . . .

Fishing Boat
Treachery Bay

12:00 am

Fireworks exploded overhead and even though the shoreline was over a mile away, I could hear the shouts and cheers even from where I was in the fishing boat. *Happy New Year*, they shouted. Yeah, I thought. New Year it might be. Happy it sure wasn't.

As our boat bobbed on the black water, yesterday's warning made me shiver. The new year seemed to loom ahead, like some monster rising up from the deep . . .

Every January since I could remember, Dad, Mum, my little sister Gabbi and I piled into the car and headed towards the coast for the beach house at Treachery Bay. But this year, Dad wasn't with us.

I looked at the guy sitting across from me —

my uncle – my dad's identical twin. Strangers couldn't tell them apart; to me, they looked completely different. Uncle Rafe's face somehow seemed harder than my dad's. Their features were identical – they were both tall with dark hair and squarish faces – but Dad often looked like he was thinking about a secret joke, while Rafe often looked like he was at a funeral. I was fair and slight, like Mum, but hoped that *I* looked more like my dad than Rafe did.

12:13 am

The wind had risen and I could no longer hear the hiss of the white-hot embers from the fireworks hitting the water. In the southwest, a huge bank of black clouds was about to swallow the moon.

"Uncle Rafe," I said. "There's a big squall coming up. We've really gotta be getting the boat back."

I was suddenly aware that all the other small boats had disappeared.

"Rafe, start the motor now. We've got to get back – the squall's going to hit any minute."

I pulled out our life jackets, threw one to Rafe and put on my own.

"Cal," he said, "don't you think you're worrying a bit too much?"

"You don't know how fast the squalls move across this bay," I spat back at him. He'd only stayed at the beach house once or twice and I couldn't remember him ever going out in a boat. "It's going to hit in minutes, trust me."

12:17 am

I'd been out in this same battered old boat with Dad since I was two. He'd taught me a lot about the estuary lakes and bays, and right now the mood was murderous. The ocean was pushing its way in—I could see the dim white tops of the rolling breakers. The storm clouds were moving fast and the night was almost pitch black. The building waves were sending our boat lurching.

The outboard wouldn't start. Rafe fumbled and muttered, trying again and again to get it going.

I hoped the waves wouldn't get any bigger. Once waves get to a certain size they collapse, and if a big one collapsed onto this little boat, it would capsize us, no question.

"Here, give it to me!" I called, as I crawled towards the stern. "Let me have a try!"

I pushed Rafe out of the way, stumbling as a huge wave lifted our boat up then dropped us.

"What are you doing?" he yelled at me.

I ignored him, too intent on getting us out of

the situation. I gripped the starter motor loop and pulled, but the engine wouldn't kick.

"It's flooded!" I shouted. "You've flooded it!"

I knew Mum would be anxious, waiting on the beach, wondering why we hadn't come back yet. Again, I tried the outboard. Nothing.

"Calm down, Callum!" Rafe yelled to me over the deafening wind. "Let's just wait it out another five minutes."

I looked at my uncle, who was drenched and unsteady. "We haven't got another five minutes!"

12:39 am

The squall surged through the ocean on gale-force winds. The tops of larger waves were breaking over the boat, and despite my frantic bailing, we were taking on water too fast.

"Grab a bucket!" I yelled. "Hurry up and start bailing, we could lose it!"

"The motor still won't start!" Rafe yelled back.

All around us were huge, shuddering sea walls, hemming us in on every side. A wave suddenly pulled the water out from under us and smacked our boat down hard into the empty trough. I hung on tightly with one hand, while still trying to bail water out with the other.

It was a losing battle. For every gallon of water my bailing threw out, ten more crashed in.

Already it was slopping heavily around my shins. The boat shouldn't be floundering like this, I thought. The buoyancy tanks in the hull were designed to keep it floating, even with a lot of water on board, even if it capsized. What was wrong?

1:01 am

The stern of the boat was now sitting low in the water, weighed down by the outboard. The front of the boat lifted, like the top end of a seesaw. Somehow, the buoyancy tanks weren't working. We were sinking.

1:12 am

Then came the rain, drenching us in blinding sheets. Rafe continued to make useless attempts to restart the outboard. At least we've got life jackets, I thought. We won't drown.

I groped around for the rope to lash us together in case the boat sank, when I sensed something nearing. I looked up and I couldn't move. It was like facing a nightmare. A monstrous thirty-foot wave was towering above us. There was nothing I could do. I heard Rafe shout out something, just before the great wall of water trembled above us, then curled over in an avalanche.

And that was the last thing I saw.

My arms and legs were ripped in all directions as I corkscrewed deeper and deeper into the seething water. My fears about rising and bashing into the underside of the hull quickly changed to absolute panic as I realized that my life jacket, suddenly extremely heavy, was dragging me deeper, and further away from the surface.

Wildly, I kicked out, struggling to free myself. I knew I could hold my breath for almost a minute. I had to make it to the surface.

In a fleeting moment, a blurry, almost-forgotten memory of my dad's face seemed to hover in the ocean above me. His eyes were desperate, he was fully-clothed and swimming down through the water towards me. And I, a three-year-old who'd carelessly slipped off the jetty, watched his terror as I sank helplessly below to the bottom of the bay. He saved me from drowning that day. He was gone, but he'd save me again. Mum and Gabbi couldn't take another death.

1:25 am

With the last of my strength, I tore off the life jacket. I kicked and stroked upwards towards a surface that seemed impossibly far away. I felt like I was getting nowhere, but I kept fighting through the crushing tons of water . . . and I pictured Dad. Then, when I thought I couldn't hold my breath one second longer, I burst through the wild surface.

1:26 am

By now the squall was at its worst. The wind lashed me with spray. I grabbed hold of the boat, which was now riding bottom up, only inches above the waves. I clung to it and sucked in huge gulps of air whenever I could get my mouth above water.

I couldn't see my uncle anywhere. "Rafe!" I screamed, spitting out salty water. But my voice came out like a whisper beneath the sound of the storm.

"Rafe!" I screamed again before being thrown around by another massive wave. This time the force of the storm tossed me to the other end of the barely visible boat. Somehow, it was afloat, and even though the surge crashed my body hard against the hull, I caught hold of the anchor rope and quickly looped it around my wrist.

1:35 am

The rope rubbed salt into my broken skin. I could only hope that Rafe was OK and making his way towards the shore for help. But in these conditions, what should have been a thirty-minute swim might have taken hours.

The boat had flipped over and trapped air beneath its upturned hull. I was lucky. While the boat stayed on the surface I had a chance.

2:59 am

I knew I must have been way out to sea now, miles from the beach. The anchor couldn't possibly hold against the violence of the storm. I shivered from wind chill and being in the water too long. I wondered if it was shock as well. My lashed hand was aching and I glanced down to find a long gash running across the back of my right hand under the rope.

Things Dad had said came back to me – I could almost hear his voice in my head: *Callum, you know what to do in this situation. Relax and tread water. A person can stay afloat for hours if they do that.* I tried to stay calm by thinking of all the reasons why I couldn't die.

I had to find out what Dad meant in his last letter. I had to see the pictures he drew while he was in the hospital – the ones that Dr. Edmundson was going to send to me. And now, the crazy guy on the street? I had to know what was going on.

4:13 am

The storm was easing. The swell was still strong and choppy, but the worst of the weather had moved on. Carefully, I lifted my body, trying to see if I could find the shoreline. I was looking for lights, but all I could see was three hundred and sixty degrees of black.

I blinked, painfully aware of how swollen and sore my eyes were. Slowly, I began to make out the shapes of the waves in the moonlight. My hand was hurting bad and I loosened my hold on the anchor rope. Blood seeped from my injured flesh.

Blood in the water.

Another flashback hit me. This time, a horrible image of a dead dog washed up on the beach . . . or, at least, the head, shoulders and front legs of a dog. It had been torn in half, and there is only one thing in the sea that can do that.

An icy fear shivered through me.

I started reassuring myself. Sharks rarely came into the estuary. Surely by now searchers would be getting ready to start looking for me at first light. All I had to do was hang on, stay with the boat, and wait for rescue.

5:02 am

It seemed as though I'd been hanging on, head

against the hull, rope around my wrist, for hours, trying to stay alert. Exhaustion was making me weak. I could barely feel my fingers.

Then something bumped into the boat, hard. I hoped we'd collided with something submerged, drifting in the water. I looked around. The sky was much lighter, but I couldn't see anything but the chopping waves.

Another bump, this time so hard I almost lost my grip on the rope. I still couldn't see anything, but I knew something was out there. I was freezing cold, but broke out in a sweat.

A third bump, so hard that it knocked me completely into the water. I splashed and slipped, scrambling back to the top of the upturned boat, hauling myself up by the ridge. In the gray light I spotted a ten-foot shark rolling over, exposing its pale belly before disappearing again.

I waited, sick with fear, praying that it had gone away. I searched around for a weapon – anything to try and defend myself.

Tossing on the waves, and just out of my reach, was the boat's gaff hook.

Yet another powerful bump and the upturned boat and I, clinging desperately above, started to move over the water. The shark was under the boat, powering us along! Any minute now, it would bash through the hull and grab me. Then, just as suddenly as it began, the motion stopped. I watched the dorsal fin speed away.

Was it leaving?

The shark had pushed me and the boat closer to the floating debris. I saw, again, the long wooden handle of the gaff hook floating nearby. And then, in the background, I saw the vanishing fin slow, turn and flick around. The shark was coming back – and straight for me!

Without even thinking about it, I seized the hook. From somewhere I was aware of a loud, throbbing noise, but I was focused entirely on the huge shark plowing through the water.

Whoomp, whoomp, whoomp. I didn't have time to think about anything but the beast before me. I raised the gaff hook, ready. The shark charged and I whacked the hook down as hard as I could on its head. Its cold left eye stared at me as it rolled underwater again.

"Come on!" I screamed furiously. "Where are you?!"

5:28 am

Not knowing where it was lurking was worse even than seeing it.

I looked up in the direction of the noise and in a brief moment of relief I saw a helicopter in the sky. But when I turned back around, I was met with the shark. And it had returned with a friend.

Through the pink-gold surface of the dawn sea, the two fins came straight at me.

The first one hit the boat. I was terrified that if I hit the shark and the hook got stuck in its sandpaper skin, I'd be pulled into the water where the second one circled.

The first shark disappeared.

"Hang on!" shouted a male voice. "You're going to be OK. Just hang on, Callum!"

I faced the circling shark, hook raised. The first shark was still hidden somewhere. There was no way I could fight off two of them.

Above me, a man in an orange coverall was being winched down from the helicopter.

"Sharks!" I screamed out. "There are sharks!"

The first shark suddenly revealed itself, coming at me with open jaws, ready to ravage. With every ounce of strength, I roared and smashed the gaff hook across its upper jaw. It dropped away and, for a second, I thought I was safe. The upturned boat lurched. The second shark was underneath me now!

"Hurry!" I screamed into the sky. The orange coverall man couldn't hear me above the noise of the rotors and the engine.

The sea flattened as the helicopter came in lower. The second shark surfaced. Now the two of them raced towards me.

Somehow, I made out the man's words. "I'm coming in close now! I'm going to grab you, OK?"

What if he missed?

What if I fell straight into the teeth of the two sharks?

I didn't know where to look – what to do . . . The first shark hit hard, gnashing its jaws, tugging and shaking the boat.

"Let go, Cal! Let go and grab me!"

The helicopter then came down so low I thought it would end up in the sea. Suddenly the shark released the boat, leaving three of its teeth embedded in the aluminum.

The voice yelled, closer now. "Grab onto me!"

The second shark knocked the boat, almost throwing me again into the water. It was now or never.

Just as I grabbed onto my rescuer, the first shark charged the boat with such force that its body skimmed over it. I wrenched myself up fast. The man tightened the rescue sling, clamped his legs around me, then swung me away to safety.

Beneath me, the sharks lunged, jaws gaping wide.

Beach House
Treachery Bay

9:46 am

I lay back and stared at the ceiling of my bedroom in our beach house. The local doctor had checked me out, stitched my hand and given me something "to help me relax." Yeah, sure. Relax.

I'd told Mum and Gabbi some of what had happened out on the boat. If only they knew about that crazy guy, back home, yesterday. Now I felt really weird – spaced out – as if what had happened overnight had been some sort of hallucination. The pain in my fingers and the gash on the back of my hand proved its reality. I remembered the sharks and shuddered, then drifted back to sleep.

5:25 pm

It was dark. For a moment, I thought I was back in the shark-infested water. The room spun. I grabbed the sides of the bed and saw my hands, raw, scraped and swollen.

Mum and Gabbi brought in some hot soup and pulled the blinds up, letting light into the room.

"Where's Uncle Rafe? Is he all right?" I asked.

Mum shook her head. I could see tears in her eyes. "There's been no word about him at all," she cried. "Why didn't you turn back before the storm? Even *we* could see the weather coming in!"

"I tried to. I wanted to," I said. "I kept telling him, but Rafe –"

"Rafe doesn't know the estuary like you do!"

"I know! But he wouldn't listen to me, Mum!"

The phone rang. "I'd better get that," she said, wiping her face and walking away.

"Don't worry about him," I called out as she left the room. "He'll turn up."

Gabbi climbed on the bed. "I hope Uncle Rafe's OK," she said. "Do you really think he's going to turn up?"

"He will. I'm sure he's fine."

"But what if he drowned, Cal?"

"Gabbi, he's fine."

I hoped what I was saying was true.

Gabbi snuggled down beside me. "I'll stay here and protect you from anything bad," she whispered.

I hugged my little sister. That's what I used

to say to her when she was really small and afraid of the dark. Now she was nine and afraid of nothing.

"Thanks, Gab. But I need to sleep."

8:03 pm

I woke up drenched with sweat from a nightmare. It was always the same one. I'm lying, unable to move – something horrible is happening – I'm freezing with cold and dread, but I can't do anything about it. And somewhere there's this threadbare white toy dog that, for some reason, totally scares me.

Gabbi came in, and I tried to shake it out of my head.

"Are you OK, Cal? You were calling out something. Three hundred and sixty-five what?"

"Oh, nothing, I was just having a bad dream."

"Uncle Rafe's OK," she said. "He washed up at Swans Nest."

I exhaled quietly.

"I'm glad he's alive, but the idiot almost got the two of us killed," I said.

"Mum doesn't think he's an idiot," said my sister. I hated hearing that.

Gabbi plonked herself on the floor, cross-legged, and looked up at me. "Why weren't you wearing your life jacket?" she asked. "The men from the helicopter said you didn't have it on."

"I *was* wearing it. It's somewhere at the bottom of the bay now."

"What? It fell off?"

"I had to pull it off. It was dragging me down. The stuff inside must have been waterlogged or something."

"I've never heard of that happening."

Come to think of it, neither had I.

Gabbi pulled off her silver and black Celtic ring and leaned up on the bed to stick it on my little finger. "Here. I want you to have this," she said. Dad bought the ring for her in Waterford and gave it to her when he came back from his first trip to Ireland.

"Hey, I can't take that from you. You love that ring!"

"No, you have it. Please? It'll keep you safe. If you're safe, I'm safe too." She lifted my hand up with both of hers. "See? It fits perfectly."

8:16 pm

There were voices outside as Rafe arrived. I could hear Mum shouting at him in the kitchen and I couldn't help but smile. It hurt my face, but it was worth it.

After Gabbi left the room, I checked out my face in the mirror. This was the first time I'd had a real good look at myself and I looked pretty shocking. I had myself a black eye, my lips and nose were skinned red raw, and my left cheek was all swollen and purple, with a long graze across it that marked me like war paint.

I looked hard at my face. It seemed different. And not just because of the cuts and bruises. It was more serious, harder, determined. I had a lot to sort out and I hoped the kid behind the face was up to it.

My dad was a photo-journalist. He'd gone to Ireland last year to gather footage for a documentary about Australian families with Irish ancestry. He was there with another colleague, researching, interviewing people and speaking at a huge conference, when apparently he stumbled onto something incredible.

I was determined to find out whatever it was that he had discovered about our family – the massive secret he'd told me a little about in his last letter, over six months ago. I'd read and re-read his words, trying to find something that would give me a clue. He'd sent me a drawing of an enormous angel too, that I was also yet to decipher.

The angel stood tall and was dressed in a full military uniform from the First World War. He held a flaming sword and his wings were partly folded, rising up above him. If he spread the wings out, he'd have a wingspan like a 747. A guy like that wouldn't flap through the air, he'd whoomp, whoomp, whoomp like a Black Hawk helicopter.

I pulled Dad's letter out from my backpack.

CLONMEL WAY GUEST HOUSE
CARRICK-ON-SUIR, IRELAND

June 2

Dear Cal,

Only a few more weeks and I'll be home and can tell you why the enclosed angel drawing is so important.

Briefly—and I need to be really careful in case this letter falls into the wrong hands— I believe I've discovered something about our family that will cause a sensation! History itself is going to be changed, if we can work out some very complicated clues. Cal, please keep this to yourself, for now, but you kids had better sharpen your wits and get used to the idea of being rich!

I can't say much more because it's not safe. There's at least one party that already knows something—a very dangerous woman who attended the conference in Kilkenny where I delivered my presentation on the Ormond family. She questioned me relentlessly and is determined to find out what I have. If she knows about it, I'm sure other people do too. Anyway, I just found out that she has underground connections...

I need to get as much information as possible while I'm here in Ireland. Your mum and Gabbi don't need to know anything at this stage, but when I come home we'll all figure out a plan of action. We need to decide how to go about keeping things quiet... until the right time.

Cal... it's so hard to write this. I really don't want to worry you, but if anything were to happen to me, you'll have to be the one to see this through. With the stakes involved, the danger could be extreme. Please promise you'll keep this to yourself. I'll fill you in on everything when I get back.

Can't wait to see you all again.

Love, Dad.

I pinned the drawing on the wall. A breeze from the window lifted the paper, making the angel look like he wanted to fly. I took him down and folded him away with Dad's letter. I didn't want Rafe seeing it.

Dad's words kept spinning around in my mind. I could feel grief grabbing me, but I bit it back. Us, rich? What had he discovered? I didn't want any more danger. I'd had enough.

I couldn't wait until the other drawings arrived in the mail. Maybe Dad drew something that would help me understand what in the world the Ormond Singularity was.

2 JANUARY
364 days to go . . .

"Cal? Cal? Are you awake?" Mum gently shook me.

"I am now."

Sunlight streamed through the cracks in the blinds and I could hear the sound of birds and the ocean. I loved the beach house, but I wished we were back home already and that I was waking up in my own bed. I tried to sit up quickly, but fell back in pain.

"How are you?" Mum asked, straightening my pillow.

"I'm pretty sore, but OK. What is it, Mum?" I asked, noticing her puffy, worried eyes.

Mum pushed her hair back with both hands. "After what you've been through, and now this happens . . ."

"Mum, what's going on? What's happened?"

"Cal," she said, all too slowly, "our house was

broken into last night."

"We were robbed?!" I asked in disbelief.

"Yes, we were robbed."

"What did they take? Do the police know about it? Did they catch them?"

Mum looked over to Rafe as he limped into my room. He had some deep cuts down one side of his face and a bandage around his left foot. "Your mother's just told you what's happened back home?"

"Yeah," I said, but shook my head.

"How are you feeling this morning, Cal?"

"I'll survive," I said. "What about you?"

Rafe looked down at his bandaged foot. "After we capsized I was washed away and spent most of the night drifting. But then I got caught up near the rocks at Swans Nest. That's when I did this," he said, pointing to his foot and the grazes on his face. "We've both had some very bad luck."

I didn't say what I felt like saying – how he'd contributed to our so-called "bad luck." Maybe he'd listen to me in the future.

"Your life jacket held up OK?" I asked.

"Fine," he said. "I can't imagine what happened to yours."

He spotted my dad's letter on the bedside table and picked it up. "What's this? A letter from Tom?"

I snatched it away from him. "That's mine," I

said, stuffing it into my backpack on the nearby chair.

Rafe shrugged and limped out of the room. "Well, you'd better have something to eat and get packed up," he called out. "We have to head back to Richmond. We've got a burglary to deal with."

Home
Flood Street, Richmond

2:21 pm

The four of us stood in shock amid the mess in our house. The place looked as though it had been turned upside down, literally—the couch and chairs were overturned, books had been knocked off the shelves and were lying ankle-deep on the floorboards. Some of the paintings and Dad's framed photographs were on the floor, glass shattered, others hung at crooked angles. The blinds and curtains had all been torn down. The place was trashed.

We were all speechless. Our home wasn't a mansion, like Rafe's enormous place, but over the years Mum and Dad had spent a lot of time making it really nice, with polished floors, high timber ceilings and tall windows opening onto the back garden. Now it looked like a garbage dump.

The kitchen had also been totaled. Plates were smashed and cutlery was lying everywhere. The doors to the garden were swinging wide open and papers from inside were flying around the deck.

"Oh help," cried Mum. "I can't believe this. What next?" She leaned over and started picking up pieces of her favorite teapot. I stood there, helpless, wishing I knew what to do. "I'll find you a new teapot, Mum," I said, trying to help her with the broken china.

"It's not fair," sobbed Gabbi, hugging Mum's waist. "What are we going to do?"

"What *can* we do but start the cleanup?" I said, grabbing the broom and throwing it to Rafe, who caught it deftly.

Mum smiled at me. "That's exactly what your father would have said."

"I'll check the grounds," said Rafe, throwing the broom right back to me, and heading for the backyard. "I'll look for clues as to who did this. Find out how they got in here."

"What about the police?" Mum asked, her big green eyes filling with tears.

"It's been a while, Win," Rafe replied, "since the police investigated house burglaries."

Maybe I should have been grateful that Rafe was there to help us. But I just couldn't. There was something about him that I didn't like. Maybe I was angry with him for looking like Dad, but not *being* Dad. He was sort of doing Dad things, like helping Mum cope through the last few months and taking over the business of the estate. But most of the time I found myself wishing he'd disappear.

"Why did they do this?" cried Gabbi "We're not even rich!"

Mum walked around, pale and silent, picking up chairs and standing them upright again. I followed her through the chaos and into her bedroom. Again we stopped in shock. All her drawers had been pulled out, and the clothes from her wardrobe lay in piles, all over the carpet.

"No!" Mum cried. "They've even gone through Tom's things!"

The suitcase that had arrived by sea mail from Ireland late last year, sent over by my dad's landlady with the rest of his stuff, lay wide open, its contents scattered. Mum hadn't been able to face going through Dad's stuff and, until now, his suitcase had stood quiet and unopened in the corner of the bedroom.

I could see some of his clothes: the big gray-green sweater he used to wear when he'd take me paragliding, his jeans, the colorful socks Gab gave him with the Disney characters on them, his flannel pajamas, and some of his old sneakers.

Mum fell to her knees and pulled the big sweater to her, hugging it and sobbing. I knelt beside her, cringing in pain from my injuries, and put my arm around her.

"Don't cry, Mum. Please don't cry." It was a stupid thing to say. I felt like crying, too. I never knew what to say to her when she was sad.

"Who do they think they are? Breaking into other people's houses like this! Turning our lives and our private things upside down! Like we haven't been through enough!" Now anger blazed on her face as she started stuffing things back into the suitcase.

"My room's like this, too!" Gabbi said, crying in the doorway.

I watched my mum pull herself together. She sniffed back tears and held out her arms to Gab. "Come on, sweetie. Try and make a start in your room," she said, "and as soon as we've finished in here, we'll come and help you."

Mum and I began the cleanup in her room. I found something lying under one of Dad's T-shirts that turned out to be an old, worn, leather-hinged jewelry box. Inside, on fraying black silk, was a deep oval indent where some large piece of jewelry must have once been. It was empty now. I showed it to Mum. "Whatever was in here is gone," I said. "What was it?"

Mum took the jewelry box from me and closely looked it over. "I don't know, I've never seen this before. Where did you find it?"

"Just here, underneath Dad's T-shirt. Must have been in the suitcase."

"Maybe what was in it has fallen out."

We searched everywhere, but whatever had been in that box was definitely gone. Mum clutched the box close. "Your dad must have bought it for me as a present," she said. "And of all the things in this house, those thieves have taken it! His last gift to me and now I'll never even know what it was!"

"The police might be able to get it back," I said.

Mum looked at me with fear in her face. "But Cal," she said, "how did the thieves know about the jewelry box in Dad's suitcase when I didn't even know about it?"

She was right. Was this the only thing the thieves had stolen from our house – or – and I thought of Dad's warnings in his last letter – had the contents of this old jewelry box been their target all along? This was quickly starting to look like something far more sinister than a break-in by a couple of petty crim' trying to make a buck.

For a moment I wondered if I should tell Mum about Dad's letter and the warnings from the crazy guy that chased me on the street, New Year's Eve. One look at her changed my mind instantly. She was far too stressed out. Instead, I went back to searching through Dad's things.

"What's this?" I asked, pulling out a sheet of tracing paper from the mesh sleeve in the suitcase.

Kilfane

Gmanagh

"What's G'managh and Kilfane?" I asked.

"I don't know," said Mum, blowing her nose. "People he met in Ireland?"

When Mum turned back to the floor, I put the tracing paper in my pocket. Something told me it could be important, like the drawing of the angel.

4:41 pm

"When I called the police," Rafe announced to us in the kitchen, "they said to make an inventory of everything that was taken. There's a chance that something stolen from here might turn up in a pawn shop somewhere later."

"Nothing's been stolen from my room," I said. As I had suspected, nothing of mine seemed to be missing. Everything looked trashed and thrown around, but my laptop, DVDs and CD player were still there on my desk.

"Nothing's gone from my room, either," said Gabbi, climbing onto one of the kitchen stools.

Rafe closed the sliding door behind him and Mum poured him a cup of tea. We'd eaten almost a whole package of chocolates left untouched by the thieves.

"That's very strange," said Rafe. "Everything seems to be in order outside, too. Apart from the laundry room door — which is where they got in."

"Rafe," said Mum, "there's an empty jewelry box in Tom's suitcase from Ireland. I don't know what was in it, or if anything ever *was* in it."

"What suitcase? What jewelry?" asked Rafe, anxiously.

I stared at my uncle, wondering why he was suddenly so interested.

"What is it, Rafe?" asked Mum, putting her tea down. "You look upset."

"How am I supposed to handle my brother's estate efficiently, Win, when I don't even know about the arrival of a suitcase from Ireland?"

"I would have mentioned the box to you if I had known about it," said Mum. "But after everything that had happened, I didn't even want to touch that bag when it arrived. It's not important, anyway. There's nothing in it that would have any bearing on the estate, Rafe. Just Tom's clothes and some personal items." Mum's voice caught on the last few words.

"But you mentioned a jewelry box!" Rafe insisted. "Any jewelry should be inventoried!"

"Well it can't be," I said. "Because whatever *was* in there is gone."

Rafe shook his head and muttered something, then limped out of the kitchen, abandoning his cup of tea. Gabbi nudged me. "What's his problem?" she whispered.

"He's always been strange," I whispered back. "I guess all of this has made him even stranger."

3 JANUARY

363 days to go . . .

11:21 am

I phoned Boges. I couldn't wait to tell him what had happened. I knew he'd be blown away.

Boges is my best friend, from school. We've been tight ever since he walked into my kindergarten class, ten years ago, with his weird hand-painted wooden lunch box and *so what?* attitude. He's Ukrainian and heaps bigger than me – heavier and more muscular – and everything about him is sort of round. We get pretty competitive with each other, but it always seems to even out. I'm lighter and faster on my feet, but he's a total brain. He tops in all of our classes, and even though he messes around all the time, he gets away with it because the teachers think of him as some sort of eccentric genius.

"Our house was broken into," I told him. "The whole place has been trashed, but I don't know if they even took anything. Nothing seems to be missing, and the one thing that we think is missing, might not have even been there in the first place."

I heard something crash on the other end of the line. Boges fumbled with the phone.

"Just a sec," he called out.

Boges cruises the trash dumps, collecting things he can fix and recondition. He rebuilds laptops, computers, cameras, phones, and gets all sorts of small motors running again. Then he sells them all on eBay and makes a fortune. He must have been in the middle of working on something complicated.

"Dude," said Boges, jumping back on the phone, "you're not making much sense. Slow it down, hey?"

I told him about the break-in and the empty jewelry box in the suitcase. "And Rafe completely freaked out about it," I said. "Like he knows something we don't."

"Your uncle has always been a freak-out kind of guy," said Boges. "At least that's what you've always told me. He's not exactly calm when you need him to be."

He was right. Rafe was pretty edgy, and a loner, too — the opposite of Dad. Gabbi and I never had much to do with him until Dad came back sick from Ireland last year. Rafe had been on vacation down south somewhere, but came back when he found out about Dad. I was starting to feel a bit guilty about my attitude again. I knew he was trying to help Mum, but I just couldn't lose that bad feeling.

I was about to tell Boges what happened after I last saw him, New Year's Eve – the crazy guy, and the Treachery Bay disaster, but I was interrupted by the arrival of our neighbors.

"Sorry, gotta go, Boges. Talk to you tomorrow."

6:42 pm

Marjorie and Graham from next door came over and spent the afternoon with us, helping with the cleanup and getting our house back to normal. They ordered pizzas for dinner, and by nighttime, the house looked pretty much the way it had when we'd locked it up last week. Mum couldn't thank them enough.

"That's what neighbors are for, Win," said Marjorie, as Mum said goodbye to her and Graham at the front door.

Rafe left to go home, too. I was watching him get into his car when I heard Mum calling me from the kitchen. "Cal, I want to talk to you."

Gabbi had fallen asleep in front of the TV, and I threw a blanket over her before sliding onto one of the stools next to Mum.

"Not too many people your age have had to experience what you went through in the sea the other night," Mum said, as we sat around the breakfast bar. "Not knowing whether you'll live or die." Her eyes filled with tears and I let her tuck my hair behind my ears. Normally we fight over my hair, and during the holidays it had grown pretty long. She paused. "With the robbery and everything, we haven't even had a chance to talk about what happened. I want to know that you're OK, Cal. Especially after everything else . . . losing your dad." She sighed. Her face looked so sad and defeated. "I want you to talk to me if anything's bothering you. Anything at all, OK? Now, let me have a look at that hand."

Mum undid my bandage and carefully lifted the antibiotic gauze off the wound. The swelling was going down already. She pulled a clean bandage out of her pocket, and looked at me, waiting for me to say something.

"Don't worry about me," I shrugged. "I'm fine."

4 JANUARY

362 days to go . . .

11:35 am

Boges was at the door. Today he had his wavy hair – which he hates – all pushed back.

"Hey," he said, his smile quickly fading from his face as he saw mine, battered and bruised. "What happened to you? Were you in a fight?"

Here we go, I thought.

"There was a boating accident on the lake," I said, "and I nearly drowned."

Boges stared at me blankly.

"I had to be winched out of the sea by helicopter. Oh, and there were sharks, too."

Boges stared at me blankly.

"Yeah, right," he said, after a moment of silence. "My gran won fifty million in the lottery. And NASA's picked me for the next moon landing."

He stood there laughing awkwardly, waiting for me to join in.

But it wasn't funny. I unwrapped the bandage on my hand and showed him my bloody gash.

Boges whistled. "How come you didn't tell me about this when you called yesterday?" he asked.

"I was going to — but then . . . anyway, you know now."

"So it was you!" Boges said, eyes suddenly wide. "No way! I saw it on the news — some kid having to be rescued off the coast!" He grinned at me. "Man, you're famous!"

"Do I want to be famous for that?"

Boges looked up at my house and the mounting pile of broken stuff near the trash cans. "How about a gangland robbery?" he suggested with a grin. "Maybe there was gold bullion in your dad's suitcase. And that's been taken, too. How would you ever know?"

"Gold bullion. Right."

We laughed. It was the first laugh I'd had in ages. I forgot my sadness over Dad for a second, before it all came rushing back at me like the sharks.

12:02 pm

The phone in the living room rang. I ran to get it, and Boges followed.

"Hey Theo," I said. It was Dad's friend calling

from the coast. "Do you want to speak to Mum?"

"No, not really," he said. "I think she's got enough on her plate. I'd rather tell you."

"Tell me what?" I asked. Already, my stomach was tensing.

"Cal," said Theo, "I've just been talking to the local police at Treachery Bay. Your dad's boat washed up a couple of miles north, early this morning. Near Swans Nest." There was a pause. "He said the boat had been sabotaged."

"Sabotaged?"

I remembered the sluggish way the boat had flopped around in the waves, and how quickly it had started to fill up, lying too low in the water.

"Yes, I'm afraid so, Cal. According to the police, someone made some very deliberate incisions in the metal. The buoyancy tanks would have slowly started filling up almost from the moment you two headed out."

"I wondered why the tanks weren't keeping us afloat. But who would do that? We could have died out there," I whispered — I didn't want Mum to overhear.

"Anyone could have done it. It's easy enough to get into the shed. Probably some drunken lout's idea of a joke. There's not much the police can do. I guess you can consider yourselves lucky."

After answering Theo's questions about how

we all were, and saying I'd pass the information on to my uncle, I put the phone down. I didn't even bother telling him about the break-in.

"What's going on? Who was that?" Boges asked.

"Something's really wrong," I said. "Something seriously messed up is happening to my family. Ever since Dad went to Ireland last year, everything's turned bad."

I showed him Dad's letter, and the angel drawing. He sat and took it all in slowly and silently. Then I filled him in on the sabotaged boat, my waterlogged life jacket, and the crazy guy and his warning about the Ormond Singularity.

"The what?" Boges asked.

"The Ormond Singularity. Something connected to my family."

"It sounds dangerous, dude. Your uncle won't be happy when he hears about the foul play," said Boges. "I hate to say it, but I don't know about Theo's 'it was probably just a couple of drunks' theory . . ."

"Theo? What did Theo want?" Mum asked as she stepped into the kitchen. She started loading the dishwasher.

Boges sat down uncomfortably.

I didn't want to worry her with the latest news. Not yet.

"He'd been talking to the cops," I said. "The boat washed up near Swans Nest and he thought we should know."

10:49 pm

Boges had gone home and I was lying on my bed, trying to get some sleep. It was such a hot night. All my bruises were aching and my hands were stinging. I stared at the drawing of the angel, remembering the last days I spent with Dad in the hospice. His body was limp and rotting, but his eyes had followed me intently.

"What is it, Dad?" I'd asked.

I'd felt he was desperate to tell me something. But by then, he couldn't speak.

8 JANUARY

358 days to go . . .

Home
Flood Street, Richmond

8:03 am

My nightmare receded as I realized that the howling wasn't coming from that dark and desolate place that had haunted me for years, but was just a passing siren.

In the past week, most of my bruises had faded, and the gash on my hand was starting to heal. My mind was reeling with unanswered questions. I wanted to know why my life jacket failed, and who had deliberately damaged our boat. Had the danger Dad talked about in his letter followed me to the peace of Treachery Bay? The crazy guy's warnings were haunting me, too. But I had survived the first week of the first month. 358 days to go.

10:07 am

After my shower I went to the kitchen to get something to eat. I heard Rafe coming down the hallway and wondered what he was doing back at our place. He walked into our kitchen with a bulging canvas grocery bag and some mail under his arm. He pulled out a loaf of bread and some whole grain rolls, and put them on the counter.

Rafe passed Mum some mail as she came in through the laundry room door. "These are for you, Win," he said. "They've been in the mailbox all night. But this one . . ." He paused, looking up at me. "I'll keep this. It's for me. It's from the hospice."

He was holding a large envelope that was thick and looked like it was filled with papers. As he slipped it into his bag I caught a glimpse of the address on the front. The envelope was addressed to me!

"Hey, that package is mine," I said. It must have been Dad's drawings, from Dr. Edmundson.

"Nonsense. It's official business. You know I'm handling the estate for your mother."

"But it's addressed to me. Look at it!"

Rafe's eyes, stern and steady, penetrated

mine. "You're imagining things, Cal," he snarled.

I stared right back at him. He had intimidated me as a kid, but that was a long time ago. "It's addressed to me!" I repeated and lunged at the bag. Rafe violently snatched it away from my reach, then lost his balance on his bad foot and fell back hard onto the floor. Oranges spilled everywhere.

"Cal!" my mum screamed at me, rushing over to help him back up. "What in the world is wrong with you?"

They both looked up at me in disgust. I didn't mean to hurt him – the idiot fell over himself. I was just about to say so, but I knew it was no use. Rafe shot me a filthy scowl as he steadied himself, then he turned to my mother. "You don't have to rush, Win," he said, ignoring me. "We're meeting the lawyer at three. I need to run some quick errands and drop the rest of these groceries off at my place. I'll catch up with you a bit later."

Rafe gathered up his oranges, tossed them back in the bag with the envelope, and left, letting the door slam on his way out.

"Cal!" Mum shouted at me again. "What is wrong with you? Why are you giving your uncle such a hard time? Do you know how difficult this mess would be for me if he wasn't around to help?"

"Mum, that envelope had *my* name on it."

She rolled her eyes. "And why would the hospice be writing to you, Cal? All the bills and other communications come to either me or Rafe!"

She paused and took a couple of deep breaths. "Look, I'm sorry, Cal," she continued. "I know it's hard for you, with Rafe doing all the things Dad used to do. But we can't change what's happened. No matter how much we don't want it to be true. This is the way it is now. You can't take your anger out on Rafe. We're lucky we have someone looking out for us."

I didn't feel like breakfast anymore, so I got up and left the kitchen.

I knew Mum'd be standing there by the counter feeling helpless, watching me walk away from her. I couldn't expect her to understand, but I knew what I had seen. Rafe was going to drop his grocery bag, with *my* package inside, back at his place. Somehow I had to get my hands on what was mine.

11:22 am

"So Uncle Rafe and I are meeting the lawyer at

three o'clock this afternoon," said Mum, who'd quietly crept up to my door. "But I'll be leaving shortly because I have other business in town. I should be home by six, Cal, but just in case I'm late, there's some lasagna in the fridge. Can you please hold the fort here until I get home?"

"Sure," I said. "We'll be fine."

"Mum, I hate it when you're home late," said Gabbi, having walked in on the last part of our conversation. She dragged her feet along the floor, arms out and head back like a zombie. "It's so *boooring* here. Can I go to Ashley's house?"

"OK, but you'd better check with her mum first."

"I already have!" said Gab with a flick of her hair.

Great, I thought. Mum out of the way. No little sister asking questions. Perfect conditions for a couple of investigators.

11:30 am

I phoned Boges.

"I need your help."

11:55 am

Ashley and her mum had just picked Gabbi up when my cell phone rang. I pulled it out and headed back to my room.

"Is that Callum Ormond?" a woman asked. I didn't recognize her voice at all.

"Yes. Who's this?"

"You don't know me, but I nursed your father at the hospice . . . He was a lovely man."

"You knew my dad?" My stomach lurched. "You're a nurse?"

"No, I'm not anymore. Look, I know this might sound a little mysterious, but I really need to meet up with you. Your father gave me something to give to you."

Dad couldn't even talk by the time he came home to the hospice. How could he have asked her to give me something? I hesitated. Who was this woman?

"My father couldn't speak by then," I said.

"That's true," she agreed, "but words aren't the only way a person can tell you what they want."

What sort of language was she talking about?

"What did he give you?"

"Well, I don't want to say too much — especially over the phone. Can you meet me tomorrow at the cenotaph in Memorial Park? Do you know it?"

I knew Memorial Park. It was on the outskirts

of the city, just over the bridge. I'd driven past it with Dad a few times and noticed the arched building at one end of it.

"Yeah, I know it."

"Could you be there at nine tomorrow night? I have to work the late shift and can't get away 'til then. I won't keep you long."

"Can't we meet earlier? Another day?"

"I'm sorry, but that's not possible. And I can't risk my job. I'll give you my cell phone number in case something happens."

"What do you mean, 'in case something happens?'"

"I just mean, if you need to contact me."

There was something odd in her voice, but I didn't know exactly what. I took down her number.

"What's your name? How will I know you?"

"My name's Jennifer – Jennifer Smith. I'll see you tomorrow."

Before I could say anything else, she'd hung up. I wasn't happy about the idea of meeting a stranger in a park at night, but if I wanted to get hold of whatever it was that Dad had given her, I *had* to meet her. I needed every possible clue to Dad's secret.

2:09 pm

I was still thinking about the mysterious call from Jennifer Smith, wondering if that was even her real name, when I picked up my phone and sent Boges a text:

📱 r u ready for job at 3?

📱 i'm in!

📱 c u outside target's place.

Rafe's House
Surfside Street, Dolphin Point

3:03 pm

"OK," said Boges as we stood outside Uncle Rafe's place. It was a modern two-story house that he moved into a few years back, after my aunt – his wife – died. He ran his drafting business there now.

"Your uncle must be loaded," said Boges, looking around at the mansions of Dolphin Point. "So what's the plan?"

"I'm going to go inside and look for the envelope. I know it had my name on it and I'm sure it's got the drawings in it that Dr. Edmundson told me about. I just hope Rafe came by and left it here. We've got a good two hours at least – by the time they meet with the lawyer in the city and then make it home."

Boges nodded, slightly distracted by a nearby bright yellow Ferrari.

"Some woman called me earlier," I continued. "She said she looked after Dad when he was here in the hospice, and that she's got something to show me. I agreed to meet her tomorrow night in Memorial Park."

"Tomorrow *night*? Who is she?"

"Someone called Jennifer Smith."

"*Someone called Jennifer Smith*?" Boges laughed. "I don't know, dude . . . Are you sure you should go?"

"I have to."

"Yeah, but it could be a setup. Don't forget your dad's warnings. He mentioned a dangerous woman in his letter, remember?"

"I know. The woman he met at the historical conference in Ireland . . ."

"That's the one. What if it's her? What will you do?"

"Run like . . ." I joked.

"It sounds dodgy to me. I'd come with you, but I'm supposed to be working."

When he wasn't studying or working on

electronics, Boges was helping his uncle and his mother, who were cleaning contractors. Sometimes he'd take on jobs instead of his mum, when her back was acting up.

"Don't worry, I'll be all right," I said. I seemed to be making a lot of promises lately that I really wasn't sure I could keep. "Right now I need you to be the outside man, here," I said, pointing at the entrance to Rafe's house. "Keep your eyes open. Try to stay out of sight, and text me if I need to get out. OK? I really don't want anyone catching me."

I threw my backpack over the iron gate, then quickly climbed up and over.

3:10 pm

I slipped into the house through the back sliding doors. I'd "borrowed" the key from Mum's dressing table.

It felt strange being there, alone in the empty house. It was such an awesome place, I wondered why Rafe never made us feel welcome. I'd only been over a couple of times, but the house would have been perfect for Sunday barbecues and backyard games, especially when Dad was around.

3:13 pm

The smell of Rafe's cigars was so thick that it was as if he was there in the next room. You'd have to feel lonely in a big empty house like this, I thought. Doubt started to kick in again. Maybe Rafe really was trying to protect me. But why wouldn't he talk to me about it? If I was old enough to take up Dad's work – whatever it was he needed me to do – surely I didn't need Rafe treating me like a kid. I couldn't make up my mind about him.

I started my search through the house, going straight for the kitchen. I was relieved to see the oranges there in a bowl on the table. The canvas bag, now empty, sat on a nearby stool. I opened drawers, felt around above the fridge, looked in all the cupboards . . . nothing.

I headed next to the huge office where Rafe worked at his angled drafting board. I looked around at his desk, his computer, the photocopier and the printer perched along the low counter. All I found were files containing receipts, orders for house plans, and drafting paperwork.

I made a quick check of the piles of paper on his desk, and when I saw the name "Ormond" written in Rafe's handwriting, on a half-hidden sheet of paper, I immediately pulled it out.

The Ormond Riddle?

The Ormond Riddle? What was that about? There were so many things in our family that might have been considered riddles. Like the mysterious viral disease that rapidly destroyed my dad, tangling all the connecting lines in his brain. Or like the run of tragedy and bad luck we'd had since his death. The warning about the Ormond Singularity and the fact that someone had deliberately sabotaged the fishing boat. The failure of my life jacket. The break-in . . .

More like Ormond *Curse*.

I turned my attention to three big red-lidded plastic storage boxes. I rifled through them, but only found old botany books, flagged with notes and diagrams, and more of Rafe's drafting papers.

The other downstairs rooms didn't take long. Under the red lid of another plastic box were Rafe's personal stuff and more books on flowering plants and ferns. Dad had told me that Rafe studied botany at the university, years ago, but I never realized how into it he was.

3:20 pm

I crept upstairs and looked around. Rafe's bedroom was right at the back of the house, overlooking the garden. Before going in there, I searched the other two bedrooms, without luck. They looked – and smelled – as if they hadn't been opened in months.

In Rafe's room I started with the wardrobe, and found lots of his jackets hanging in an orderly row. All of the pockets were empty.

Next I checked his chest of drawers, but once again, found nothing. There was no sign of the envelope anywhere.

What could he have done with it? I wondered. What if he still had it with him and this whole sneaking in thing had been a waste of time?

I had to keep moving. All that was left to search were his two bedside tables. One was piled with history books, with some medical bill sitting on top. The drawer beneath revealed only handkerchiefs, a half-used box of cigars and a travel guide. I looked over at the other bedside table. My last hope. Once I'd checked that, I'd be out of there.

3:29 pm

📱 GET OUT NOW!

Was Boges joking?

Surely Rafe and Mum would still be at the lawyer's?

I ran along the hallway and looked out the window.

Rafe was walking up the driveway!

Immobilized, I stood still, my mind frantically trying to work out what to do. If I bolted, I might just have made it down and out the back doors before he'd make it upstairs. But if I did that, I'd never know what might lie in the unsearched drawer.

I ran back down the hall to Rafe's bedroom. I had to find out.

I fell to my knees and wrenched the drawer open. And there it was! The envelope *was* addressed to me – with the name of the hospice in the top left-hand corner.

I quickly snatched it up. I needed to run, but I stopped, immobilized again, staring at what I had found lying underneath the envelope. I'd never seen one so close before. Carefully, I lifted it out, mesmerized by its blue-black steeliness. It was so much heavier than I'd imagined. The weight of it, and the four-digit serial number punched in its left side, made me pretty sure that it was no replica.

What would Rafe need this for?

Get a move on, I told myself, and turned back to the envelope, noticing that it had already been opened. It looked thinner than when I'd seen it before. Inside, as I suspected, was the letter from the neurologist. But no drawings.

There was a noise downstairs.

Rafe was already in the house!

I stuffed the letter back into the envelope. I hoped Rafe'd stay in the living room so I could sneak out the front door.

I strained to listen to his footsteps so that I could tell where he was and what he might be doing. But then I heard his heavy limp coming up the stairs.

Desperately I looked around. There was no way I could get out. If I ran down the hall, I'd collide with him at the top of the stairs. I had to hide. I shoved the envelope back in the drawer and closed it. The only place that offered some cover for me was the narrow area between the wall and the other side of the bed. I hurtled over and dropped to the floor, trying to squeeze myself under the bed. It was too low and there was no way I was going to fit, so I just lay there flat on the floor, pressed close to the dusty carpet, praying that if he came into his bedroom, he wouldn't see me . . .

I held my breath and tried to calm my pounding heart. Louder and louder his footsteps sounded until I knew he was in the room. Then, through the narrow gap between the base of the bed and the carpet, I saw his black shoe and the bandage on his other foot. I tried to make myself even smaller and flatter. What was he doing?

A tickle of dust in my nose made me twitch. I couldn't afford to sneeze. Not now. I pressed my lips together, too scared to breathe. And what I'd seen in Rafe's bedside drawer a moment ago made my anxiety burn so much stronger.

Uncle Rafe seemed to just stand there. He was taking something from the bedside table. I hoped it wasn't my envelope.

I watched the black shoe and the bandaged foot turn away as Rafe walked across the carpet towards the door. As he vanished through it, I heard something small fall on the bed. He'd thrown something back in the room.

The footsteps descended the staircase.

I realized I'd been holding my breath and exhaled in relief.

I waited until I heard the front door open and close again. Slowly I crawled out.

There was a key on the bed. It had a black tag and looked like the key to a front door. It was familiar, but I couldn't remember why. I picked it up and put it in my pocket, then turned back to check the bedside drawer again.

The bill that had been sitting on top of the history books was gone. It must have been what Rafe had come back for. I opened the drawer again, expecting to find the envelope gone, too, but it was still there. It was then that I noticed something else was missing . . .

3:44 pm

"Why didn't you stop him? He nearly found me in there!" I dragged Boges out from the corner of the garden. He'd been hiding behind a bushy tree.

"He was walking up the path before I even noticed him! You said he'd be gone for ages! What was he doing back here anyway?"

"Must have forgotten a couple of things. Picked them up and went out again. He dropped this." I held up the key.

"What does it open?"

"Not sure."

"Well, he's gone now," said Boges. "Heading towards the city again. You look like crap. Did you find the envelope?"

"I found it. Addressed to me. The letter from Dad's doctor is in there, but the drawings are missing. You won't believe what else I found in there . . ."

I took a deep breath.

"My uncle has a gun."

3:49 pm

Boges blinked at me. "A gun! Why? What would he have a gun for?"

"I don't know, but he took it with him. I'm telling you, you can't trust that guy. I'm going back inside. Can you wait here for me?"

3:57 pm

I went straight back to the bedroom, and this time I took the letter from the envelope and hurried downstairs to the photocopier.

We first met Dr. Edmundson when Dad was flown back from Ireland and admitted to the neurological clinic. Later, when they moved Dad to the hospice, Dr. Edmundson visited him daily, still hoping to unravel the mystery and diagnose the deadly virus.

St Luke's Hospice

Dear Cal,

When we were cleaning out the room after your father's death, a staff member found these drawings and remembered how Tom had insisted that you should see them. This nurse had been able to communicate with him in a very special way. I've been meaning to send them on to you ever since. I must apologize for having delayed so long. I would have given them to your uncle earlier but I'm ashamed to say that when he was here making the final, sad arrangements, I couldn't find them. They were stuck in a file that I've just only now sorted through. I believe they were the last drawings your father was able to do before the disease completely destroyed his motor coordination.

These drawings were important to your father and he wanted you to have them. He would have known what they meant, even if he could only convey the meaning in this displaced way. I'm sure he hoped that you would be able to work out what he was trying to say.

Again, my apologies for keeping these drawings for so long. I know they will be very precious to you and your family. In a way, they are your father's last gift to you all. If you can work out what they mean, I'm sure they'll be a very great blessing. Tom was a fine man, a great photographer and outstanding journalist. You can always be very proud of him.

My best wishes to your mother and the rest of the family.

A nurse? Was it Jennifer Smith?

I looked up from the letter, recalling how the doctor had explained things to us last year.

"Tom can still call on abstract concepts – or ideas that in his mind are related to what he wants to convey – even if we don't know what the connections are," he'd said. "He's lost the usual ways – speaking and writing – and we don't quite know why this is. Your dad isn't going crazy. He's using whatever brain connectors the virus has left him, and it's like a code that we can't always understand. Just yesterday, when Tom wanted a book, he drew his reading glasses. It's like he can't come directly to what he wants, but he can draw something related to what he's trying to say – something at least one or two steps removed from the actual object."

I had to find those drawings and work out what they meant. I pulled out the key that I'd picked up from the bed and stared at it. I knew I'd seen it somewhere before.

My sense that Dad needed to tell me something in those last few weeks, returned in full force. In the days before he died, with Mum and Gabbi sitting close by, softly talking to him and holding his hand, I would sometimes climb right up and onto the bed and lie beside him, my head on his chest, listening to his heart beating. In those moments, I had the strongest sense that he was trying to tell me something, trying to tap it out. Something urgent. A warning.

The words on the page blurred as tears began to fill my eyes. But I had to hold back — I had a job to do.

I replaced the letter in its envelope and hurried upstairs, putting it back where I found it. I stared again at the space where the gun had been.

What would Rafe have done with the drawings? And what did he need the gun for? Did he need protection, or did somebody else?

Boges's House
Dorothy Road, Richmond

4:58 pm

We wheeled our bikes onto the narrow front porch of Boges's old row house, leaning them against the wall near the front door. Boges pushed it open and we went inside.

Today, his gran was asleep in the first bedroom, just visible through the partly open door. She was lying on a sagging bed, snoring softly. She'd never really left the old country, Mrs. Michalko used to say. And sometimes I'd hear Boges speaking to her in Ukrainian, like he did with his mum. Boges was the only male in his house, same as me, now.

Boges opened the freezer and pulled out a popsicle.

"Hey," I said, holding out my hand. "Where are your manners?"

He grabbed another and tossed it to me.

Once in his room, we pushed the old beanbag out of the way.

Boges read the photocopy of the doctor's letter. He handed it back to me without saying a word.

"The specialists said that as Dad got worse," I explained, "the connections in his brain stopped working properly so he couldn't say or write what he meant – all he could do was draw." I paused, wondering whether I should continue. "I really think he was trying to tell me something important. He wrote me that other letter I showed you, before he got really sick, back when he was in Ireland. But by the time he came home, his mind was all shot. See, I had this massive feeling, especially at the end when Dad was almost completely paralyzed . . . He'd lock onto me with his eyes and they'd follow me as I moved. Dr. Edmundson said it was just a mechanical movement – that Dad's eyes automatically followed moving objects. I – I don't know. I think there was more to it."

Boges started scratching the back of his head. He wasn't often lost for words, but the head-scratch had become a dead giveaway.

"Do you think this nurse is the woman that called you?" he asked.

"Could be."

"What exactly was your dad doing in Ireland?"

"He was there for the conference, but he was also researching family history – not just our family – for an upcoming TV series on some Irish families and how they lived from medieval times right up to today."

"Genealogies," Boges nodded. "Like how some have been successful while others have kind of died out."

"Right," I said.

"So while he was researching he found out something incredible about your family. But what?" Boges looked hard at me. "The drawings *are* important," he said. "They are the way in."

"The way in? To *what*?"

"That's what we're gonna have to work out. But we have to find them first."

6:11 pm
_____

I kept thinking about Dad all the way home. It

was early Tuesday night, and normally, when Dad was alive, I'd have on my Air Cadet uniform and we'd be driving out to the airfield. I was hoping to have my private license in a few years. Those days were over. Now, everything had changed – and so had I.

Home
Flood Street, Richmond

6:19 pm

I went straight down to my room and put the letter and the key away, and then I heard Mum come home.

I went out to the kitchen.

"How are you feeling, hon?" she asked.

"OK," I said, still thinking about my conversation with Boges. "Mum, before he got sick, did Dad tell you anything about discovering something about our family?"

"What do you mean?"

I wasn't sure what I meant really. "Something unusual? Something that might – I don't know – cause a problem?"

Mum looked puzzled. She shook her head. "Not as far as I know. Why do you ask?"

"Oh, it's nothing. I was just wondering about the time Dad spent in Ireland, doing that family research stuff. What did the lawyer want?"

Mum sighed. "Just more documents to sign. Your dad wasn't very good at organizing his business. It's a bit of a mess, really."

Mum suddenly started crying, holding onto the counter with one hand, pushing tears out of her eyes with the other.

I put my arms around her. "Mum," I said, "tell me if there's anything I can do to help."

"Oh Cal, some days I'm OK. Other days . . ."

"I know," I said. "Me too."

She blew her nose and straightened up. "I asked Rafe about that envelope you wanted."

"And?"

"He said he could see that it was official paperwork from the hospital, so he just took it. He didn't want to worry you."

"Did he say what was in it?"

"Just some medical reports, apparently. Copies of the last tests that Dr. Edmundson made. For the UVI – you know, the unknown viral infection, that killed your father."

Liar.

"Well, did Dad ever say anything to you about something called the Ormond Riddle?" I asked.

"Who told you about that?" Rafe's voice made me jump. I swung around. He'd crept in behind me, quiet as a cat, and was standing in the doorway, just like Dad used to, wearing Dad's face as if he'd stolen it and put it on crookedly.

"No one. I just heard about it."

"Where?"

"I dunno." I shrugged, trying to look ignorant.

"I want to know where you heard about it!"

"Rafe?" Mum interrupted. "What's the matter? What's with the interrogation?" She tried to make a joke of it, but Rafe glared at me. Did he know about me busting into his place?

"I just saw something about it on the Net," I lied.

"Come on, Rafe," Mum said, "everyone's still a bit touchy. Sit down and let me get dinner on."

"Thanks, Winifred. I don't mean to sound like an interrogator, but I'm worried about you, Cal."

"You have been through a lot," said Mum putting her hand on mine, while flashing a look of approval at my uncle.

"Uncle Rafe is only trying to be helpful, aren't you, Rafe?"

"That's right, son."

I looked at him and his eyes were cold. I nearly said, "I'm not your son," but I shut my mouth. I knew it would just upset Mum. I hurried to my room and picked up Dad's last letter from Ireland, before going back out to the kitchen. Mum and Rafe were whispering about me, I was sure. They both looked up when I announced, "I'm going out."

"Where, out?" Mum asked.

"Boges's."

"But haven't you just come back from there? What about dinner?"

"I'll have it later," I said as I slipped out the door.

Boges's House
Dorothy Road, Richmond

6:41 pm

"He's a liar!" I said as soon as Boges opened his front door. "He completely lied to Mum about what was in the envelope he pinched!"

"That proves it, then."

"Proves what?"

"How important the envelope is. How important the drawings are. Your dad said that his discovery would change history – that's a big claim, my man, and those drawings are your only hope right now. They're your dad's last will and testament. To you."

"What could he possibly have found out? The crazy guy kept warning me about the Ormond Singularity," I said. "What is that?!"

"I don't know. But it sure sounds like something that could put your family in danger. The stakes are always high when there's big money involved."

Big money. I never thought my family would have anything to do with something that involved big money.

"Maybe Rafe thinks that he should have been sent the drawings, not me," I said. "And so he kept them. Mum always used to say that he was jealous of Dad."

"Jealous? What of?"

I shrugged. "Dad was always the stronger twin, older by a few minutes, and Mum reckons Uncle Rafe always resented him when they were growing up. Sibling rivalry, she called it."

"He might have taken a look inside the envelope on his way into the house," said Boges, "seen the drawings and decided to keep them. He might have told you about them later. Now we'll never know."

I didn't want Rafe working out the messages in the drawings before us. But at least I had the tracing paper, with the names G'managh and Kilfane, that I found in Dad's suitcase. Rafe didn't know about that. Not that I had any idea where that fitted in, or whether it fitted in at all.

I didn't know what was going on with Rafe. All I knew was that I didn't trust him.

Home
Flood Street, Richmond

8:30 pm

After I reheated my dinner, Rafe got up from the paperwork he was looking over with Mum, and followed me to my room.

"Feeling more yourself?" he asked. "Like your mother says, you've been through a lot lately." His eyes scanned my room: my desk, my walls, the mess on my floor.

I mumbled something instead of saying, "If you'd listened to me at Treachery Bay, I wouldn't have been through quite so much."

"It's very important, Cal," he said, "that you remember where you heard about the Ormond Riddle."

"Why? What is it with this riddle anyway?"

"It's — er, it's of historical interest. To me. You know how interested I am in the family . . . and family matters."

That was news to me. Rafe never had much to do with us, until Dad died. And even on the rare occasions that we did see him, he was always going on about how Dad should get a real

110

job – with a newspaper, keeping regular office hours, instead of whizzing all over the world chasing weird stories. Dad would laugh it off, even though Mum, Gabbi and I would be sitting there wanting to tell Rafe to shut up. Dad was the one that was always trying to keep the family together. He was the one interested in our family. No matter what.

"Try the Net," I suggested, thinking I'd do the same.

Rafe stood there for a moment, staring at me. I turned away and started eating my dinner, hoping he'd get the point. Finally he walked away, leaving me even more suspicious.

CONSPIRACY 365

9 JANUARY
357 days to go . . .

Memorial Park
Venetian Way, Richmond

8:56 pm

Everything was telling me this wasn't a good idea. I'd convinced Mum that I was going to see a late movie with Boges. If only he wasn't working tonight.

"I wish you'd stay home and have an early night," Mum had said. "But I guess it's school vacation – you can sleep in tomorrow."

I glanced at my watch . . .

9:10 pm

She should be here, I thought. I didn't like the look of the dimly lit Memorial Park ahead of me. Being there seemed crazy. I was starting to feel edgy. A jet roared overhead and I concentrated hard on the dark mass of the cenotaph.

I didn't hear the car behind me.

I turned, but it was too late . . .

9:14 pm

"Hey! What's —"

My words were muffled by a hand over my mouth. Someone else tackled me. I lashed out, kicking and cursing, but no sound could get past the vicious grip across my face.

Two men hauled me up against the car — it looked like a dark blue Mercedes — and threw a heavy sack over my head. My arms were wrenched behind me and tied up tight, then I was lifted off the ground and tossed like garbage into the trunk.

"Who are you? Where are you taking me?" I shouted, trying to tear my arms out of the rope.

"Keep still, and you won't get hurt," one of them hissed at me. He pushed me down and then slammed the trunk shut.

9:19 pm

I tried working out where we were going, and in what direction, from all of the bumps and turns, but soon I was hopelessly disoriented. I was shaking. I should have listened to Boges. He knew it was a setup.

I remembered seeing something on TV about a girl who was kidnapped and thrown into a trunk – she somehow kicked the back lights out, squeezed her arm through, waved it around frantically, and eventually grabbed someone's attention. I tried desperately to do the same, but I could hardly move in there. I was squashed up against something else – something big and lying behind me. I couldn't kick my leg out far enough to even bump the lights.

I thrashed around, frustrated, trying to free myself from the sack, when a loud thumping came from inside the car.

"Keep still in there!"

10:02 pm

It felt like we'd been driving around for ages, and when the car finally slowed and pulled up I had no idea where we were. The sack slipped a little as I was dragged out of the car.

"Come on, Buster," said the guy who'd thrown me in the trunk, a huge barrel of a man, with a bald head and an earring. I caught a glimpse of a sandstone curb, a large front gate, some tiled steps, and some bushes and trees. But before I could note any more details, the guy pulled the sack back down and I was pushed up the steps ahead of him.

UnKnown Location

10:09 pm

I stumbled into a room, tangled in the sack. All I could see were some red and black tiles and people's shoes.

"What's going on?" I shouted, scrambling to my feet. "What do you want with me?"

"What do we want with you?" said a woman's voice. I wasn't sure if it was the same voice I'd heard on the phone – it could have been.

"Let's see," she said. "We want to know about the Ormond Riddle."

There it was again, those words I'd seen scribbled in Rafe's office.

"We want to know everything," she said, "so you'd better start talking."

"Answer me!" she screamed, kicking the back of my knees. My legs buckled and I fell to the floor.

"I don't know anything about the Ormond Riddle! I don't know what you're talking about! Why don't you ask someone else called Ormond? There are heaps of us. *I* don't know anything!"

And it was true. I didn't have a clue. But these guys weren't buying it.

"I'll ask you a different question," continued the woman's voice. "What do you know about the

Ormond Singularity?"

"Look, I don't know anything about that either!"

"You must!" she yelled. "Tell us what you know!"

"I don't! Just let me go, you're wasting your time!" I tried to stop my voice shaking – I didn't want these people to know that I was scared. What if they killed me and buried me in the backyard? Nobody even knew where I was. *I* didn't know where I was! Boges only knew about Memorial Park.

My interrogators changed tack.

"What do you know about the Ormond Angel?" The voice was now slow and serious.

"Nothing."

Boges was right. The angel *was* important.

"We'll start again," my interrogator said. "We've got all the time in the world."

"No, we haven't," I heard someone whisper behind me.

"Shut up, Kelvin," said the woman.

Someone seized me by the shoulders and lifted me up. "Tell us what you know or things are gonna get real nasty around here."

I thought things were pretty nasty already.

10:31 pm

"For the last time . . ." someone started to say.

"I thought you just told the little punk that we had all the time in the world."

"Shut up, Kelvin!"

"Tell us everything you know about the Ormond Riddle and the Ormond Angel."

"What are you talking about?! Nothing! I know nothing about either of them! You have to let me go!"

But they were relentless. On and on they demanded answers. I rolled around, on the floor, being pushed and kicked and shoved. My hands were still tied and I was still trapped inside the hessian sack. I was sweating, panting, and everything was muffled.

11:29 pm

I told them I had to go to the bathroom. One of them led me there, pulled the sack off my head and slammed the door shut. "Tell me when you're done," he yelled from outside before bursting into a fit of laughter — probably on realizing how much I'd struggle having my hands tied behind me.

I looked around, but there was no way out.

There weren't any windows or vents. I tried to mentally take down notes about the space I was in and then I flushed the toilet with my elbow. Before I could yell out, the door swung open, the sack was thrown over me again, and I was dragged back for more questioning.

"Your father gave you a map, didn't he." It was spoken like a statement, not a question.

"No," I said. "My father did not give me a map. I don't know anything about a map. A map for what?"

"Your father —"

"My father has been dead for over six months!" I yelled. "He couldn't even speak by the time he came back from Ireland! How could he have given me a map! Figure it out already — you're wasting your time on me! I don't have anything you want!"

In the silence that followed my outburst, I could hear a whispered conversation going on among my captors. I caught some of the words. It sounded like these people had been at the conference in Ireland. They must have heard about the Ormond Riddle then. And the Ormond Singularity — whatever it was.

11:58 pm

Without any warning, I was dragged down a hallway and shoved into a small room, not much bigger than a cupboard. I was leaning over to shake off the sack, when a heavy blow to the back of my head floored me.

10 JANUARY

356 days to go . . .

12:29 am

I was lost in some strange, black and painful dream world. Faint voices floated around me.

"We've already wasted enough time on him. He doesn't know anything."

"He's useless. We should just let him go."

"But we've got to get rid of him!"

"Throw him off the Gap?"

They were going to kill me! Throw me off a cliff!

"Can't you see he's more helpful to us alive than dead?"

"But he could ID us. We don't have a choice. He has to go."

"No. We need him alive."

12:38 am

The voices slowly faded in and out. I lay on the floor trying hard to stay alert, fighting the heaviness in my head. I tried to focus on what the voices were saying. It was all so hazy. I was feeling around for the walls to try and prop myself up, when the door suddenly opened. A dark, blurry figure leaned in towards me . . .

5:51 am

Slowly I woke up. I had no idea how long I'd been out for, but figured it must have been a good few hours – it was starting to get light. I didn't know if the voices I'd heard had been real or just part of some delirious unconsciousness. They felt like a distant memory. Had someone been in here, too? I wondered. What had happened?

My shoulder was throbbing and I guessed I must have bashed it hard on something when I was knocked out before. It took me awhile to clear my head and get my balance. I shook the sack off and took a look around.

Whether the voices were real or not, I had to find a way to break out of there.

6:01 am

I'd been imprisoned in a sort of closet, a tiny room where cleaning things were stored. I could barely move with all the mops, buckets and junk covering the shelves and floor.

As my eyes adjusted, I noticed a skylight in

the roof. I desperately looked around for a way to get up there, but first I had to free my hands. I needed something sharp.

6:07 am

I had a plan. I pressed my ear against the door and listened carefully for signs of movement on the other side.

Silence.

In the doorway, a broken tile jutted out. Its edge was rough and sharp. I turned around and positioned my tied hands over it, then began rubbing them back and forth, trying to cut through the rope.

It was painful leaning back in that position, especially with my aching shoulder, and no matter how hard I tried, I couldn't cut the rope without cutting my hands too.

It hurt, but the plan was working.

6:13 am

My hands were free. I looked up again at the skylight. It seemed impossibly high, but I had to try and get up there. I quickly upturned a stack of mop buckets, steadied them, and then using the corners of the walls to help me, I climbed up on top.

Crouching uncomfortably, and supported by the

walls, I slowly straightened up. I couldn't afford to fall — the sound of all those crashing buckets would bring my captors running, for sure. This had to work.

For a second I thought I heard something outside, but it might have simply been the ringing in my throbbing head.

6:19 am

They were back! I had to move fast.

"There's nothing to connect him with us," I heard a man say. "We have to keep him here, for now, but later we'll let him run then grab him when we need him again."

Were they going to hunt me down like hounds chasing a fox? Hearing that gave me all the motivation I needed. My fingertips barely touched the edge of the skylight, but it was now or never. I bent my knees a little, and then launched at the rim of the skylight. For a moment I thought I would fall and come crashing down, but my grasp held firm. The tower of buckets was going to topple over and give me away any second.

Braced against the wall, supported with one arm, I felt around for the handle of the skylight. I pushed with all my strength. Nothing. I tried again, pushing harder, and this time it creaked.

I froze. Had they heard it?

I couldn't hold on much longer. Every muscle in my body was braced to keep me up there, wedged into the corner near the ceiling, like some human spider.

Despite my unstable footing, I took a risk and with everything I had, I twisted the handle hard. And this time, with a sharp creak, the skylight opened. I made another lurching thrust and grabbed both sides of the skylight. I kicked hard against the wall and the buckets and pushed myself through the opening. The buckets tipped and collapsed, crashing hard on the floor below.

I was out. I scrambled across the roof, not daring to look behind me – the shouting below had already started. I found a balcony, jumped over and skidded down the drain pipe. Just as I leapt off and landed, a man ran out on the balcony. He looked down and glared at me. "You'd better keep your mouth shut!" he yelled, as he swung his leg around the pipe.

I turned and ran. I concentrated on running and running only, forcing myself beyond anything I'd ever done before . . .

6:58 am

I was in a strange part of town, trying to find my way home. I didn't think I could take another step, but I pushed on.

I don't know how long I walked. I wished I'd paid more attention to the house I'd escaped from. But I just wanted to get away as fast as I could and the minute I hit the ground, I'd run like a lunatic. I was sure we'd been in the car last night for an hour, at least, but maybe they'd circled a few times to throw me off.

Eventually, I came to a familiar main road, which led me home.

Home
Flood Street, Richmond

7:43 am

Everyone was still in bed by the time I got back. I crept to my room and made a few notes, jotting down the names of streets and buildings I could remember passing. There'd been a little church at an intersection not far from the house, a school and a carwash.

Then I pulled out Dad's drawing of the giant angel. I studied it hard, trying to find something in it that would give me an idea of why I'd been kidnapped and interrogated. What is it about you, I asked the stern figure, that everybody wants to know? What secret do you guard?

It was then that I noticed that the commando angel had something beneath the gas mask that hung around his neck — it looked like a decoration. Some sort of . . . medal? How could I have overlooked this before?

Maybe one day I'd find out the secret, then I could go back to that place on *my* terms.

9:21 am

I woke up and last night's terror started to smother the nightmare I'd had again. The darkness of my dream — the freezing cold, the fear, the white toy dog, and somewhere, a baby crying — was overshadowed by the memory of the closet I'd been locked in.

What was I going to tell Mum? I was sure she'd be mad at me for not coming home last night, but there was no way I could tell her about being abducted. Not after all the things she'd been through. I knew that somehow I'd just have to keep it to myself. For now, anyway.

There was a strange atmosphere in the house. I got out of bed and headed down the hall.

Gabbi and Mum were both in the kitchen, Mum on the phone with her back to me, taking down notes with a pencil.

"What's happened?" I asked, wondering if they'd somehow found out about where I'd been.

"What is it?" I asked again.

"It's *all* gone," Gabbi whispered. "All of it!"

"What? What's gone?"

Mum dropped the pencil she was using and it rolled on the floor. Slowly she put the phone down. When she turned to look at us, I gasped with shock. She almost looked as sick as when she'd heard the news about Dad's illness.

Gabbi turned to me. "All our money's gone, Cal! Dad withdrew just about everything when he was in Ireland!"

I looked to Mum as if to say, "Tell me it's not true!"

"She's right," Mum whispered. "There were months' worth of house payments left in the account. There's nothing now."

I couldn't speak. I stood watching Mum comfort Gabbi, holding her close, smoothing her hair, telling her it was going to be all right.

Without money, how would Mum be able to pay the mortgage? Until last year, she'd worked full time for an architect, but had to take a lot of unpaid leave when Dad was sick. Now she just worked a part-time job.

"It's all gone," said Mum. "Gone. Over one hundred thousand dollars has simply vanished. Our entire life savings. There are nineteen dollars left in the account."

The only sound was Gabbi's stifled sobs. I wanted to say something, but I had no words. I knew the mortgage payments on the house were automatically deducted every month from Dad's account. But what would happen now? Mum barely earned enough to pay for the groceries. We'd lost our father, I'd come close to losing my life, and now, it seemed, we were going to lose our house.

Who was doing this to us? Any lingering notion I might have had about telling Mum what had happened to me last night evaporated. There was no way I could load her up with more worry. She was so stressed that she didn't even ask me where I'd been.

"I'll have to call Uncle Rafe," said Mum.

"We won't lose our house, Mum. I can get a job," I said. "I'll leave school and look for work."

Mum grabbed me and held me in a hug. "You will not! Somehow we'll find a way through this. Thank goodness for you kids," she said, "I don't know how we're going to manage, but at least we've got each other."

Boges's House
Dorothy Road, Richmond

10:52 am

It was hot on my bike – it must have been almost ninety in the shade.

As soon as I got to Boges's we went down to his room and I threw myself on his old beanbag. I told him all about the night before and then filled him in on the news from the morning.

He sat there scratching and staring at me in disbelief. Again.

"You nearly drowned. You get kidnapped. And now your house is on the line. Is that what you're really telling me?"

"Right," I said. "I didn't think things could get any worse."

"Plus, your dad makes some massive discovery and warns you of danger, just before he gets really sick. And then some lunatic on the street chases you down trying to tell you that your dad was murdered." Boges started laughing. "Man, this is all insane!"

"I know!" I laughed back. "It *is* insane, but true!"

I couldn't believe it myself, but I was living it. A year ago my biggest concerns in life were math exams, football, girls, my little sister pinching my things, and Mum and Dad not letting me stay out late enough. How did everything change so quickly?

"You have to go to the cops," said Boges. "Cal? Are you listening to me?"

"I can't. Boges, I just can't."

"Why not?" he said, like I was crazy. "This is massive. Dude, you were kidnapped! Thrown in the trunk of a car! Locked in a closet! Knocked unconscious!"

"I can't, all right?"

I knew it sounded like the most logical thing to do, but I didn't want to involve the authorities. That guy on the balcony told me to keep my mouth shut.

"They don't want me to talk. Believe me. I don't trust them. What if they know where I live? They weren't afraid to hurt me, Boges. Any of us could be in danger. And Mum," I continued, "she can't handle this – not now. It's too much. She's already on the edge."

Boges shrugged. "I really hope you know what you're doing. Anyway . . . your dad must have had a breakdown and then taken out all of the money. Maybe it was the virus?"

I nodded, glad he wasn't pushing the cop thing. "But what could he have done with it all?"

"I don't know, but the quicker we can work out what's going on, the quicker we can sort out this mess."

He was right.

"I keep wondering," he continued, "about your uncle. Maybe *he* took the money. He *is* your dad's identical twin. It wouldn't have been hard for him to pose as your dad."

I shook my head. "The money was withdrawn in Ireland."

"OK. But he *did* lie about the drawings, remember? Why would he do that?"

It didn't take much thought. "Obviously, he doesn't want anyone to know about them."

"My thoughts exactly," said Boges. "Seems he doesn't want anyone to even know about the *existence* of the drawings. Which means they are crucial — important enough to pinch, and important enough to lie about." Boges swiveled around on his chair to face me. "It means," he continued, "that Rafe knows those drawings mean something. He knows something about the Ormond Riddle thing, too."

My mind felt like mush. I didn't think I'd ever be able to concentrate again. Too many things were happening to my family and they were all bad.

"Last night," I said, "that's all they were talking about. What do you know about the Ormond Riddle? What do you know about the Ormond Angel? What do you know about the Ormond Singularity? I kept telling them I don't know anything! Except that for some reason they all have our family's name stuck to them! Then they started going on about a map. Did I know anything about a map? Had Dad given me a map? On and on! I had nothing to tell them, but they didn't believe me. I don't know what might have happened if I hadn't gotten away . . ."

"They wanted to know about a map?" asked Boges. "How do you think they even know about these things?"

"They were at the conference in Ireland. I could hear them talking about it. I guess they found out whatever Dad did about our family."

"Your dad said there was going to be danger," said Boges. "He was right!"

I hadn't realized until last night just how dangerous this might be. Hide out, the man on the street had said. Lie low until midnight, the 31st of December, this year.

"And I don't know how much Rafe knows about all of this," I said. "Ever since the day of Dad's funeral, he's been so . . ." As I recalled moments of that terrible day, I put my hand in the pocket of my hoodie.

"Boges! I've just remembered!" I held up the key with the black tag. "I know what it opens and I know where the drawings are!"

12:43 pm

We jumped on our bikes and sped off.

"Cal, please tell me why we're going to the cemetery."

"The key opens the Ormond vault," I called out to him. "It's where my dad is, along with my grandparents and a stack of other ancient Ormonds, going right back to 1878. All of us end up there."

"You guys have a mausoleum? Creepy . . . So, all the coffins and ashes are stored there, instead of being buried?"

"Yep."

The way things were going, I thought I might be joining them early. That fear made me pedal harder. I was going to survive this. I'd carry on my dad's work and unravel the huge secret he'd stumbled on.

Crookwood Cemetery
First Avenue, Crookwood

1:25 pm

The key felt sticky in my sweaty hand as we hurried in through the heavy iron gates. The cemetery was a peaceful place with trees and small gardens intersected with footpaths. All around us were graves, some like low garden beds with just a simple headstone, while others were more elaborate with angels perched on pedestals, stony wings outstretched. I wondered if the Ormond Angel was among them. I didn't think so. I was with Mum and Rafe when we placed Dad's ashes on a shelf in the family mausoleum, and I knew for a fact that there was no watchful angel there.

The somber, stone, windowless building with its solid iron door, corroded by the weather, stood cold before us. In the stonework, above the door, was our family name and coat of arms, also weathered by wind and rain.

"Hurry, man," said Boges. "I can see a uniform heading this way. Must be security."

I stepped up the stairs, pushed the key into the lock and tried to turn it. It wouldn't budge.

"Hey, you two! Get away from there!" called out the guard.

"Come *on*, dude. Hurry up!" said Boges.

"I'm trying!"

I finally got the lock to turn and started to push the door open.

"Get out of there! What do you think you're doing?"

With the half-open door behind me, I turned to confront the cemetery guard.

"It's OK," I explained, holding up the key. "We're family."

The security guy had come right up to the mausoleum steps. Even though he was standing two steps below, he was still taller than me.

"Only the legal custodian of this grave has right of entry. Show me your certificate."

"But his father is in there," Boges said. "He has every right —"

"He has no right! He could be anyone claiming that. You two better make yourselves scarce." He pulled out a portable radio. "You can leave now, I can have my partner down here to drag you two out, or I can call the cops. What'll it be?"

I pushed the door open further and caught a glimpse of the long shelf where my grandfather's coffin lay, but there was something else there. Something that certainly hadn't been there when I'd last stepped through the door.

The security guard grabbed me, pulling me down the steps. He slammed the iron door shut behind me. Now his partner had joined him — a stocky, mean-looking man with a red face.

"Get out of here before I call the cops. Bernie?"

Bernie grabbed Boges. "They're probably just a pair of ghouls checking out a place to live."

"Ghouls?" I asked in disbelief.

"Weirdos who break into the big tombs and camp in them. Nasty sickos that we have to dispose of," said Bernie, tightening his grip on Boges.

"Get off me," said Boges, shaking free. "We're going."

1:49 pm

The security guys watched us as we unlocked our bikes and took off. I slipped the key back into my pocket.

"That was a waste of time," said Boges.

"Not quite. I saw something in there."

"Right. A ghoul," Boges laughed.

"No, I saw a large plastic container with a red lid – exactly the same as the ones I saw in Rafe's house. He's using our vault as a storeroom."

"I'd love to know what he's storing in there," said Boges, as we neared my street.

"I think I know," I said.

Just before we parted at the corner, I dangled the key in front of Boges. "You know we're going back there," I said. "To make sure."

"When?" Boges looked hesitant.

"When there's no one around." I said.

"I don't like where this is heading."

Home
Flood Street, Richmond

2:23 pm

The first thing I noticed when I walked in the house was again how unusually quiet it was. Mum had left a note on the fridge.

Gone shopping.
Be home a bit later.

Fish & chips ok for dinner?

xx mum.

I stood in the kitchen listening to the silence. It was the silence of something coiled up in hiding, motionless and ready to attack.

"Gabbi?" I called. "You here?"

No one answered.

"Gabbi?" I called again.

Nothing.

I walked further into the house, cautious now, ready to run.

What I found on the floor near the kitchen made me drop my backpack.

Uncle Rafe . . . lying in a pool of blood.

2:26 pm

I rushed over to him. He was unconscious, and blood seemed to be seeping from the back of his head. Had he been shot?

I ripped open my backpack, thinking my beach towel might stop the bleeding. I was about to call an ambulance when an awful thought struck me. If Uncle Rafe was injured, then Gabbi too might be . . .

"Gabbi!" I screamed, running down to her room. "Gabbi?"

My little sister's name froze on my lips.

There she was, lying in the doorway of her bedroom, crumpled like a broken doll.

I fell to my knees, my ear to her chest. She wasn't breathing!

"Gabbi!" I pleaded. "Talk to me!"

I panicked, trying to remember how to do

CPR, like we'd been taught at school. Short, sharp bursts of pressure on her chest, pinching off her nose, breathing into her mouth. My fingers trembled, and I tried to calm myself down by remembering to count slowly between each breath.

"Start breathing!" I cried, watching her body exhale the breath I'd just blown into her. I wanted to call an ambulance, but I couldn't leave my sister alone and cold on the floor.

2:29 pm

"Breathe, will you!" I shouted at her. My heart was pounding. Gabbi couldn't die! Violent sobs shook me. Was she responding? I watched her chest — I could swear it was rising by itself now. I pushed tears from my eyes. She had to be OK!

I heard something downstairs.

For a second I thought it might be Mum and I was about to call out when I heard the voice again.

It wasn't Mum!

"Search the house," it said. It was a man. "He's in here somewhere. When you find him, make sure he doesn't get away."

It was my kidnappers and they were after me!

"Please, Gabbi," I begged, puffing another breath into her, counting and depressing her chest, "Don't die on me!"

Time was running out. Footsteps were climbing the stairs. Then I heard the sound of sirens coming towards our house. A voice on the stairs called out, "Somebody's called the cops. We've gotta grab him and get out of here!"

I searched my sister's face, desperate for a sign of life. Then, I saw the faintest blush of color and a tiny pulse throbbing in her neck. She was breathing again! And her heart was beating! I heard an ambulance siren. It was almost here. Gabbi would get help. Gabbi would be OK.

I dared not stay a second longer. I kissed my little sister on her forehead and I squeezed her cold hands. I grabbed my backpack and hurled myself through the window and into the nearby mulberry tree.

2:37 pm

The dense leaves hid me from view and I stayed there, clinging painfully to the tree. The search in the house continued. I realized I was shaking and prayed desperately that no one would see me. I pulled my backpack closer.

I'd assumed it was the people who'd grabbed me in Memorial Park. But I was wrong. It wasn't them. Who were these people?

"Look! There he is!"

I'd been spotted. I could hear them at the window.

"Up there! He's in the tree!"

Oh no he's not, I thought, and let go.

The branches slowed my fall a little, but I hit the ground hard.

I jumped over a black Subaru that was parked outside the house, and took off, running for my life, putting as much distance between me and the shouting I could hear behind me, as my pursuers tried to keep up.

A quick glance back. Two burly-looking men attempting to cross the road against the traffic, and an ambulance and cop car skidding onto the driveway.

I thought I'd run my best speed last night, but now I broke my own record. I raced across the road. Cars blasted their horns as they braked. Drivers swore at me, but I didn't care . . .

3:06 pm

I'd thrown them off now, and I was hurrying down streets I'd never seen before. I ducked into a huge shopping center where I found a quiet corner, and, panting and sweating like crazy, I called Boges.

"Boges!" I gasped, trying to catch my breath. "Something really bad's happened at home and . . ."

But Boges interrupted me. "Our place is crawling with cops! Mum's freaking out!"

"Cops at yours? Why?"

"You're asking *me* why? Look, Cal, I can't talk now. I'll have to call you later, OK?"

"No! Wait! What's happened? Why are the cops at *your* place? Boges? Please!"

But he was already off the line.

I didn't know what to do. I tried calling Mum on her cell phone, but it went to voice mail, so I left a message. "Mum, I hope you're OK. When I came home earlier, I found Uncle Rafe unconscious on the floor, his head bleeding, and Gabbi – Gabbi wasn't breathing! I did what I could and she was coming around, but I had to get out fast and . . . there are these people after me and I've been meaning to . . . " I stopped. Mum would think I'd totally lost it. I'd have to sit her down and tell her the whole story now: about how the boat had been sabotaged, about being abducted and interrogated. "I'll call you later," I said, hanging up.

3:58 pm

I sat in a coffee shop, in the corner furthest from the door, keeping an eye on passers-by. I'd ordered a drink, but felt sick thinking about my little sister lying on the floor. Would she have died if I hadn't come in when I did? Was she OK now?

I tried calling Mum again and once more it went to voice mail. I left another message, asking her to call me as soon as she could. She was probably at the hospital by now with Gabbi and Uncle Rafe. I felt choked up with anxiety and fear. Someone was targeting our family. This was out of control.

I had to make a decision. I hated the fact that those thugs knew where we lived. Maybe they'd met Dad at the conference – or just looked us up in the phone book. I knew they could come back at any time.

There was no way around this. I'd have to go to the police – tell them the whole story. Once the cops knew everything, they'd see that my family and I were in great danger.

I could tell them about the mysterious Ormond Riddle, maybe get them to help us find out what the Ormond Singularity was, and clear this whole mess up.

I could feel my confidence and strength returning. Our family would be helped.

Yes, that's what I would do.

All I had to do was find a police station.

I turned the corner a few blocks from home, past
the big hotel where Dad sometimes used to go
with work friends. That was back then, when the
world was normal, when Dad was alive and my
family was safe. I distracted myself by looking
in through the doorway of the hotel lobby, my
eyes drawn to the huge plasma screen that filled
most of the far wall.

I blinked.

It was me.

My face filled the giant plasma screen . . .

The camera moved to a senior police officer.
"Police have not yet released the names of the
victims," he announced. "The first, a man aged
in his forties and believed to be a close relative
of the alleged offender, is expected to make a full
recovery. The second victim, a girl aged nine,
also a close relative, is in intensive care. Police
are warning the public not to approach the
suspect, but to call the police if he is seen. He
has already seriously attacked two people and
could be dangerous if approached."

They were talking about me!

They were showing *my* face as the attacker!

I moved quickly, head down, hurrying past the
hotel, hoping no one would look up and see me.

Around the corner, I started running. I'd have

to get home. To Mum. Explain it all to her. She could go with me . . . to the police. Together, we could sort it all out . . .

I slowed to a fast walk and became aware of a car cruising along beside me. A sideways glance – and I freaked out. It was a squad car!

I made a quick left-hand turn into the nearest street, running like crazy. The police car accelerated and screeched around the corner.

I made another sudden turn down a narrow alley and scrambled over the nearest fence, falling into a big mess of hydrangea bushes. I crouched motionless, squashed against the fence, sweating in the heat, hoping they couldn't hear me panting, and then finally the squad car sped past me in the alley. When I could no longer hear it, I climbed back over the fence and headed home.

5:28 pm

I flattened against the wall of the house on the corner of my street, peering around cautiously.

I jumped back fast. Police were everywhere! Two detectives stood outside in the garden of my place, while other officers in navy blue coveralls swarmed around in the street outside.

Another squad car blocked the other end of my street. There was no way I could make it to the house.

"Hey! You!"

I'd been spotted again!

I turned and ran.

"There he is! After him!"

I bolted, pelting along as hard as I could, jumping over trash cans, scrambling cats, until I'd come to the corner at the other end of the street that joined ours in a right angle. But instead of turning and following the street, I continued straight ahead, jumping a low brick wall, and hurtling through the garden of a small cottage, down the side passage, over the gate and straight on through the garden at the rear of the house. I threw myself over the back fence, falling heavily to the ground on the other side.

I was in the backyard of another small cottage, not far from a clothesline. I waited there for a while, listening to my heart rate slowly ease. I switched my phone off and looked around in disbelief. Here I was, hiding out near some stranger's laundry, while the police hunted me.

I was trapped in a nightmare.

Any second now, I'd wake up, safely home with my family.

6:16 pm

There was no waking from this. This was my new reality — I was a hunted fugitive.

I huddled there until nightfall. I could smell dinner cooking and watched the lights come on and off.

9:33 pm

Finally, I crept out, cramped and hungry. In the garden shed near the bushes I'd hidden in, I found an old brown rain jacket. I shook the dust and spiders off it, and in spite of the hot night, pulled it on. I climbed over the fence again and back onto the street.

I started walking.

The bright lights and the busy people of Liberty Square comforted me a little. With the collar of the rain jacket pulled up around my face and my cap pulled down, I hoped I wouldn't be recognized.

The smell of food from the nearby cafes was making me hungry. I sat down with my backpack in a park near the fountain and searched through all its pockets. I had exactly three dollars and forty-five cents. If I wanted food in the morning, I'd have to get to an ATM. But if I did that, and the police found out, they'd know where I was.

I stopped searching for money and sat with my head in my hands. Mum would be out of her mind with worry. And what about Gabbi? In intensive care! Was she going to be OK?

I switched my phone back on and it rang almost straight away.

I snatched it up.

"Cal, thank goodness you're all right!" cried my mum. "Where are you? You must come home!"

"I can't, Mum! Everyone thinks I attacked Gabbi and Uncle Rafe! What's going on? Why would they think I did it?"

"Darling, we can talk about that, later, OK? Please, just come home."

"Did you get my message? When I got home, Gabbi and Rafe . . . they were both unconscious. Gabbi wasn't even –"

"Yes, darling," she cut me off. "Whatever you say. Just come home. Please Cal, this is too much, just come back!"

Whatever you say? What was wrong with her?

I could tell from the way Mum was talking that she wasn't listening to me.

"Is Gabbi going to be OK?" I asked.

"We all hope so. Now please just come home! I've got to go back to the hospital now. But I'll be home in an hour or so. Wait for me there."

She hung up. I could hear the stress and the tears in her voice. Poor Mum had no one to help her. Now she didn't even have me.

I was about to text Boges to meet me at Liberty Square, but if the cops seized his cell phone they'd come straight for me!

I'd have to think of something.

Last year, we found a twenty-dollar bill in the bushes near the fountain. I'd ask him to meet me there. Boges would know what I meant.

📱 meet me at 10 where we found the 20.

Fountain
Liberty Square

10:04 pm

I was so happy to see Boges. I called him over to a secluded spot in the park.

"How's Gabbi?" I asked, pulling him out of the light. "I know she's in the hospital. Mum said –"

"Look man, what's going on? You're in so much trouble. I probably am too – Mum thinks I'm asleep in bed."

"Gabbi?" I reminded him. "And Mum? How is she? Is Uncle Rafe OK? Was he *shot*?"

"Hey, slow it down! Yes, Gabbi's in the hospital. She's in pretty bad shape, but she's going to be OK, OK? And your Uncle Rafe's in the hospital, too. Yeah, he was shot, but he'll survive. Your mum is all right – under the circumstances. But you'd better tell me what's going on? What did you do?"

"Do? What do you mean? I didn't *do* anything! I came home and found Rafe bleeding on the floor and Gabbi wasn't even breathing!"

I pushed away the burger he was offering me. I couldn't eat. "Why? What are they saying I did?"

"Man, I *know* you. I know you'd never do anything to hurt the Gabster. But that's what everyone's saying you did. I thought you might have had a fight with Rafe, that ended in . . . oh, dude, I don't know."

I was too shocked to say anything for a moment.

"I thought it was my kidnappers in the house, but it wasn't. When I came home I . . . I got Gabbi breathing again! I didn't hurt her. Why would I hurt her?"

"Apparently she said something about it when she was picked up by the paramedics. She screamed out your name, before falling unconscious again. And that's not all. Rafe says he thought he heard your voice, upstairs, shouting at Gabbi, and then when he went up to see what was going on, he was shot! He managed to crawl down the hallway before passing out."

I could hardly believe what I was hearing.

"You'd better eat something. You look sick."

I picked up the burger, then put it down again.

"Look, I know what's been going on, and I know you'd never do something like that," said Boges.

"But everyone else does, apparently. No wonder the police are after me. And that explains why Mum was so weird on the phone. But what is she thinking? And the bad guys were probably shaking Gab, demanding she tell them where to find me." I felt so sick, thinking of my poor little sister, wanting to protect me. "She probably knew it was me they were after, and only screamed my name to warn me . . ."

I felt dizzy so I crouched on the ground.

"I'll find a way to clear your name." said Boges. "Don't worry. You can count on me."

I tried to smile. "But who would have done this to a little girl," I added, "and to Uncle Rafe? I know something's up with him, but even so. Maybe he sensed that he needed protection, rightfully so, and that's why he's been a bit strange."

Boges finished his burger and licked his greasy fingers. "Maybe it's all part of their plan — whoever they are. Get rid of the whole family. They're dangerous and determined."

"The cops came around to our place," he said,

after a pause. "They thought you might be hiding there. They wouldn't believe my mum when she said you weren't. They want my phone and I'm sure they'll want my hard drive, too." He stood up and walked towards the fountain, then came back, kicking a stick out of the way. "They said they could confiscate any item that might be helpful to them. Said it was now an attempted murder investigation. Possibly even actual murder."

"Murder?" I said. Then it hit me. The police were thinking ahead. In case Gabbi died.

I jumped up. I couldn't bear to think of that.

Boges must have seen my face because he put a hand on my arm, and he's not a touchy-feely kind of guy. "Gabbi's going to be OK. She's a little fighter. Of all people, you should know that! Remember the day she almost KO'd you when you told her you'd donated her Jelly Babies CD to the school fair?"

I nodded, almost smiled. "Then how am I going to contact you?" I asked, despairing.

Boges grinned and pulled out a cell phone I hadn't seen before. "They don't know about this one," he said, giving me the number. "And if they take my hard drive, they won't find anything. I can fix up another one pretty quick – I just need a motherboard."

"I'll contact you again when I've got somewhere to hide out. And when you come, please bring some clothes and some money. And I'll need a flashlight, candles, and matches too. Thanks, Boges," I said.

But there was something else I needed to tell my friend. "You'd better be careful, too, Boges. It's only a matter of time before the people who are after me connect the dots and start coming after you. Once they discover you're my friend."

Boges blinked. "I thought the cops were bad enough."

"I'm really going to need your help."

Boges didn't hesitate. "Man, you've got it."

We swapped clothes and although Boges's shorts were too big for me, I pulled them tight with my belt. Boges looked ridiculous in my shorts—they were way too small for him – but he didn't care. I gave him the old rain jacket as well.

"Great start to the new year," I said. "This is all because of the missing drawings and whatever was taken from that jewelry box," I said. "We've got to find those drawings. Boges, you know we've got to go back to the cemetery, right? We have to go tonight."

11 JANUARY

355 days to go . . .

Crookwood Cemetery
First Avenue, Crookwood

12:28 am

Boges and I crept through the gloom, passing the tall cypress trees that lined the cemetery's walls. Clouds scudded across the sky, blocking the moonlight so that once we turned down the road leading to the cemetery gates we had to find our way with the narrow beams of light from our cell phones.

"I have to say, this is not my idea of fun," said Boges.

"It's not about fun. It's to get into Rafe's secret storage box."

This cemetery raid was at least taking my mind off what I'd found at home earlier.

"Once we get hold of those drawings," I said, "I'm sure we'll have a better idea of what Dad found out in Ireland."

"Right. That's if the ghouls don't get us first."

The gates were closed, but we scaled them easily enough, although I had to help Boges haul himself over. We dropped onto the other side, and crept low in the dark. I hoped no one had seen us and that we hadn't been picked up by any surveillance cameras.

"OK," I said. "No one around. Let's go quietly down to the vault and check it out."

"And then let's get out of here. This place gives me the creeps."

I was with Boges on that. In the gloom, the marble columns and angels formed ghostly figures around us.

"Hey! What was that?" Boges hissed, suddenly grabbing my arm.

"I didn't hear anything."

"Listen!"

I did, standing still. After about fifteen seconds of silence I gave Boges a shove. "Come on. You're spooked, that's all."

We were almost at the Ormond vault. I could see its bulk in the cold light of the moon which was suddenly sailing brightly above, freed for the moment from the heavy cloud. We hurried over, climbed the couple of steps to the front door. Boges shone his cell phone light onto the lock while I twisted the key in it. The door loudly creaked open. We listened, afraid security might have heard something, and then squeezed through the opening. The air was musty, cold and very still.

"I'd better wait here . . . in case anyone comes," whispered Boges. He was a smart guy, but his gran had told him far too many Ukrainian ghost stories.

I guided the beam of light around the four shelves in the front section until it fell on the carved wooden box Mum had bought. "Hi Dad," I whispered. "Just here to pick up the drawings you wanted me to have."

Then I directed the light onto the plastic storage container on the floor, squatting beside it, clicking open the handles.

I found the drawings straight away. They were sitting right on top of everything. I didn't even look at what else was in there, I just grabbed them. My excitement mounted as I lifted them out. I was aware that Boges had crept in and was peering over my shoulder, curiosity overcoming his concern about spooks. I looked at the first one. It was the angel again, the Ormond Angel.

"Let's get out of here. Grab them and let's go," said Boges.

I folded them carefully and stashed them in

my backpack.

"This is not a cool place to hang out," Boges said, as he cautiously shone his phone into the dark recesses of the vault, revealing the stairs to the lower chamber. "I didn't know it had another level."

He took a couple of hesitant steps further into the mausoleum as I stood up. "Looks full down there," he said.

"That's right. All the really old coffins, from generations ago, are stored down there. Come on. We've got what we came for. Let's get outta here!"

1:43 am

Boges went home, leaving me with the drawings. Now I was searching for somewhere to hide – safe from prying eyes. I wanted to find a place to stash the drawings and grab some sleep. All my life I'd taken so much for granted. Right now, I'd have done anything to be in my bedroom at home.

3:51 am

I wandered the streets for ages, avoiding eye contact with everyone, and keeping well away from any police, until I found myself outside a row of old houses – dumps now, but probably mansions in their day. One of the biggest houses at the far end, I had noticed, had been turned into a backpacker hostel.

Many blocks down the road, and when I was so tired from walking that I thought I'd just have to curl up under a tree like a cat, I noticed a "For Sale" sign attached to number 38, a semi-derelict mansion with a very overgrown front yard.

I took a closer look. The windows downstairs were boarded up and the front door had strong planks nailed diagonally across it. It seemed deserted.

I crept up quietly to the front door and around the porch. One of the side windows wasn't fully covered by timber and I was able to get my hands around the lowest piece, and after a struggle, pry it free.

No one could see me there on the side porch of the old place. It took awhile, but once I had the first piece of wood off, the others came away more easily.

I climbed inside, dragging my backpack through behind me.

When my eyes got used to the darkness, I could just make out old-fashioned wallpaper, stained and discolored, hanging off the walls of the room. Cracks of light from the streetlamp outside helped me to see that two old broken chairs leaned up against the front wall, and dirty old newspapers littered the floor. In one corner there'd been a staircase, but it had rotted and all that remained of it was a few steps going nowhere against the wall. The rest was a pile of broken timber collapsed beneath.

I didn't want to explore any of the dark areas until daylight, they were probably full of rats. It was a miserable place – neglected, alone and falling apart. But it would do for now.

I sat down and sent Boges a text with the address to his secret phone, reminding him to bring along the things I'd asked for. Then I curled up in one corner and fell asleep.

Hideout
38 St Johns Street

11:04 am

Someone was trying to get in the front door!

Jolted awake with panic, I skulked over to the door and squinted through a crack.

Thank goodness. It was only Boges. I whispered to him to come around to the side of the house.

He handed me a computer bag and climbed in through the window, looking around.

"This place is pretty cool. For a dump."

He walked around, carefully feeling his way, suspicious of the sagging floorboards. "There's a hole here," he called out. "It goes right underneath the house."

I came over to see. Lucky I hadn't fallen through there last night when I was creeping around. I put my head down and looked in. I could see some of the stone and brick piles that supported the house, and a whole world of spiderwebs and dust.

"Hey, the water's still on in the bathroom!" Boges called, as I lifted my head up again, hearing the sound of a flushing toilet.

"Wish I'd known that last night," I said.

I carefully made my way over the floorboards to join him in what remained of the bathroom.

The sink was broken, and the shower head was missing, but the stained toilet still flushed. Boges turned a tap on and rusty brown water dribbled to the floor. I could get a bucket and put it under the sink and wash under what was left of the shower pipe.

"Man, you wouldn't believe the hysteria you've caused," said Boges. We were sitting out back on the small porch, overlooking the tangle of vines and bushes that filled the yard.

"My mum won't quit hassling me about it. It's been on the news again, and look here . . ." He pulled out his cell phone and passed it to me. I snatched it.

> ## MISSING SCHOOLBOY WANTED FOR ATTACKS
> Police are searching for
> Callum Ormond, 15, of Richmond.
> Ormond, who disappeared
> last night after a vicious
> attack on his uncle and
> younger sister, is wanted
> for questioning.

"Great," I said, handing the phone back. "I've always wanted to get my name in the headlines."

"Even Mr. Lee, from school, was on the news!" said Boges. "He was going on about how you'd always been popular, a good kid and a good student, and that he was shocked and devastated to hear you were involved in the attacks. Then Susie Miller jumped in beside him and said something like, 'Yeah, me and Cal dated in, like, Year 8, and I just feel so lucky that the relationship, like, ended when it did. It could have turned real ugly.'" Boges laughed. "She's the only thing that's turned ugly!"

What could I say? The situation was ridiculous. I couldn't believe that I was going to have to convince my mum that I had nothing to do with what had happened.

Boges had brought me more food and drinks: water, bread, a few cans of baked beans, some chips and chocolate.

Rations.

I grabbed a bag of chips and pulled the drawings out of my backpack, spreading them out on the floor.

"Your dad sure could draw," said Boges after a while. "Look," he said. "Another angel."

It was the second drawing of the commando angel — he was smaller than the one I already had, but wearing the same World War I tin hat, and the same gas mask around his neck.

"Was your dad religious?" Boges asked, staring at the figure of the angel.

"He didn't go to church much," I said, "if that's what you mean."

I recalled conversations I'd had with Dad, especially out in the boat — we'd talk about the hugeness of the ocean and the sky, the sun blazing over the dark blue sea, and the gulls hanging on the wind. Maybe, Dad said, we can expand our minds like the expanding universe we live in. He said that life was his religion too. You needed to live it well and honestly, being grateful for whatever came along, because everything that happened was life happening, whether we liked it or not. I wasn't too sure that I understood him.

"Why would he draw an angel then?" Boges asked, "And to draw him twice?"

I looked closely at the angel's unsmiling face. He didn't actually look stern, like I'd thought at first. It was more the look of someone who didn't have any time to waste.

Someone on a mission.

"The doctors told me that Dad's mind could only work around or near the ideas he was trying to draw."

"You mean by drawing an angel he might have meant the devil?"

I shook my head. "No. It wasn't opposites. It was more of a *close to*."

"OK," said Boges, tapping on the next drawing. "What do you make of this one?"

It was a picture of a waiter, wearing a bow tie and carrying two playing cards on a tray – an ace of hearts and a jack of clubs.

"Did your dad play cards?"

"Sometimes," I said, "we'd sit around in the summer at the beach house playing board games and the occasional game of cards."

The third drawing was a collection of smaller, odd sketches. It looked like Dad had just been doodling, trying his hand with various objects. There was an old-fashioned watch on a chain, a pair of sunglasses, a ribbon tied in a bow, some flowers attached to a hair comb and something that looked like a medallion on a chain. All I could make out on the medal was some decorative leaves and scrolls around its edges.

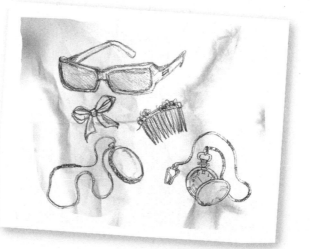

We turned to the next picture – a white-looking monkey with a fancy collar around its neck, and a fancy ball in its hand.

"Why would he draw that?" Boges asked. "And this one," he said, picking up the fifth drawing.

I took it from him, studying it close. It was a sketch of the Sphinx from Egypt, crouching in the sands, staring blindly from its blunt, eroded face.

"Did your dad ever work in Egypt?" Boges asked.

"I don't think so," I said. "I don't remember him ever talking about Egypt."

In front of the Sphinx, almost directly in the middle of the huge figure's granite lion paws, there was the bust of some Roman guy.

"So who's this supposed to be?" he asked. The figure looked serious, and had the folds of a toga over his shoulder.

"No idea. A Roman emperor?"

"And this one?"

Boges pointed to another drawing, a child with a rose.

I shook my head again.

The last drawing looked like an old-fashioned cupboard door, with some fancy carving on the top and a great big metal ring at the front. At the top of the drawing was the number five in an oval.

"Mean anything to you?" Boges asked.

"Nope."

"What about the number five?"

"Nope."

"This one with all those odd things on it – the watch, the ribbon, the sunglasses, the medal thing, the comb – reminds me of one of those 'what-do-all-these-things-have-in-common' kind of intelligence tests."

"You're right," I said, grabbing the drawing from him. "Even though they're all different, they're all things that people can wear. So what do you think it means?"

"Actually," said Boges after a pause, "I don't know."

I punched his arm and laughed. "Well we have to work out what they mean. We've already made a start."

I remembered the time Dad's old wind-up clock crashed from his desk and burst open, scattering screws, metal plates, little gear wheels, its hands and a long, blue-black springy coil. Dad's drawings were probably like that. Crazy random images, exploding out of a breaking-down mind.

I felt that Dad was still here, in his drawings, talking to me, sending me his messages. But would I be smart enough to work them out? That was the part I wasn't sure about. Even with Boges's help I was sure it was going to be a tough job.

"Rafe is going to find out they're missing next time he goes to the mausoleum," I said.

"I've already thought of that," said Boges. "He's going to think he's lost the key first. Then he is going to have to get a new one. That gives us a bit of time before he realizes they're missing. And then, we know that at least one other party is after them. Your kidnappers."

"You think he might believe that the woman and her mates have gotten hold of them?"

"If he already knows something about the

Ormond Riddle and enough about the Ormond Singularity to pinch these drawings, he probably knows that he's not the only one who's after the secret. There's no reason for him to think of you straight away."

"I wonder how he got onto it at all."

"Probably your dad told him. They *are* brothers."

"Yeah, I know. But they've never been close. Dad didn't mention anything about telling Rafe. In fact he warned me against speaking to anyone about the angel, or the secret."

Maybe Rafe's interest in the drawings was simply because he was Dad's identical twin – but my instincts kept telling me something else. I'd heard about twins who finished each other's sentences. What if Uncle Rafe had some sixth sense, some kind of special twin connection with my dad, even if they weren't close?

"There's a lot about Rafe that I don't trust," I said.

"Let's start with the angel," said Boges, straightening the drawings in a row in front of him.

He switched on his laptop and we checked out images of angels on the Net. There were a lot of angels out there, pretty ones in pink, scary ones like the Valkyries, and the fallen angels. We found some pretty amazing angel stories, but we didn't find anything like the commando angel.

3:14 pm

At least we'd found some meaning in the collection of objects and the fact that the angel, presumably the Ormond Angel, had been drawn twice. But what was that telling us?

We searched around for a secure place to hide the drawings and lucked into a good spot inside one of the large, old fireplaces. Several loose bricks came away easily and it didn't take long to brush out the soft, sandy mortar behind them. Then we pushed the drawings, along with the tracing paper with the two names on it that I'd taken from Dad's old suitcase, into the wall cavity, replaced the bricks and stood back. No one would ever think to look there.

"That sheet of tracing paper with the names on it," said Boges, "do you think that could be some sort of map? Those guys were asking you about a map, weren't they? What if this is what they were talking about? Like those names – G'managh and Kilfane – could they be place names?"

"You could be onto something! But what sort

of map has just names on it? You need places and roads and stuff as well."

"Guess so. Have you tried calling your mum again?" asked Boges. "She's really worried about you."

"Yeah, she begged me to come home, but I can't do that now," I said. "How can she think I hurt Gabbi and Rafe?"

"I don't get it," said Boges, picking up his bag. "I'm real sorry, Cal, but it's getting late and I have to get going before anyone starts asking where I've been."

"You can get out of here by crawling under the house," I said, pointing to the hole in the floorboards. "That'll take you to the front jungle."

"Think I'll use the glamour exit," said Boges, heading back to the window he'd come through. I really wished he didn't have to go.

"So how long do you think you're going to be here?" he asked, looking around at the old room with its curling wallpaper hanging like old shrouds. "What are you going to do?"

I had nothing to say. I didn't know. But I had to figure this mess out so that I could protect my family. The bad guys were still out there.

13 JANUARY

353 days to go . . .

11:00 am

I sat staring at the floor, wondering what in the world I was supposed to do to get myself out of this situation. I felt completely lost.

I'd started trying to clean up the place a little, but gave up after sweeping out the piles of dead flies and rat droppings. What was the point?

I couldn't open any of the windows for fear of being discovered, but I decided it was safe enough to leave the back door open to let the breeze in.

It was a relief to wash under the broken shower and, feeling a little refreshed, with my surroundings looking slightly better, I opened a can of baked beans and ate them cold, with chocolate for dessert.

So this is life on the run, I thought.

I pulled the drawings out again and spread them on the floor, studying them for hours, trying to make sense of what my father might have meant when he drew them . . .

16 JANUARY
350 days to go . . .

9:59 am

I'd spent the last couple of days hidden in the house, studying the drawings. But I needed money and I had to get out. I jumped on a bus, took a seat at the back, kept my head down and my cap pulled low. It felt good to be out, just another kid traveling by public transportation. I took another bus that went way out of the city, to an ATM in a suburb I hardly knew. I withdrew some of my savings. If the police traced the withdrawal, they'd think I was hiding there instead.

I looked around and saw a police car cruising down the street. Instinctively I jumped into a doorway, waiting for it to pass. Eventually the police car sped up and left, and I kept walking.

All the way back on the bus, I worried about Mum and my sister. I wondered how much longer I could live like this.

17 JANUARY

349 days to go . . .

11:31 am

Twice, street people – a couple of old drunks and later a man and woman with gaunt faces – had tried to break in, but I'd replaced the boards on the side window by nailing them from the inside using half a brick and some old nails I found in a jar. The back door still had a sliding bolt that I used to lock it up. If necessary, I could make a quick getaway by crawling through the hole in the floorboards to under the house. I'd also found a piece of carpet to pull over the hole.

My shoulder was still sore, but the gash on the back of my hand had become a dark pink scar by now. Sometimes I'd look at it and remember that night out on Treachery Bay. It seemed like months ago now, but if I could get through that night OK, I could get through this.

I'd bought hair gel, temporary tattoos, scissors and some fake piercing studs. By the cracked and blistered mirror in what was left of the bathroom, I hacked at my hair, shortening it and plastering it down. I smoothed the temporary tats onto my forearms and stuck the fake studs on — one just under my lower lip and the other on my left eyebrow. I'd already lost a bit of weight and when I finally checked my reflection, I didn't look much like the kid in the newspaper anymore.

I stared at the unfamiliar image in the mirror. I felt lonely and miserable and so angry that Mum believed I could have hurt Gabbi. I had to try and convince her of my innocence. I turned on my phone and called her.

"Mum?"

"Cal! Where have you been? What are you doing? For heaven's sake come home!"

"I can't, Mum. It's too dangerous for me. And I don't just mean the cops."

"Just come home! I've been going out of my mind with worry about you. Where are you? Where are you staying? Who's looking after you?"

"It's OK, Mum. I'm taking good care of myself. Please don't worry. Look, let's get this straight right now. I came home and I found Uncle Rafe unconscious and Gabbi not breathing. I didn't touch either of them."

"Cal, Rafe heard your voice. Gabbi was screaming out, 'No! Cal! Please, Cal, don't!' Those were the last words she said before we lost her to the coma."

My mother's voice trembled, and before bursting into inconsolable tears, she whispered to me, "And the police found your fingerprints on the gun, Cal."

Frightening images of the last few days began to flash across my mind like an out of control torture slideshow. Storms, sharks, Memorial Park, the thick weave of the sack over my eyes, the angel, the crazy guy, the cemetery vault, Gabbi lifeless on the floor, the blue-black steeliness of the gun . . . Rafe's gun.

2:15 pm

"What gun?" I demanded. "Stop crying and tell me what you're talking about!" I shouted at my sobbing mother.

She seemed shocked at my tone and her sobbing slowed.

"Cal, your uncle was shot," she said, in a serious and slow voice. "The gun was left behind. It has your prints all over it."

"That was Rafe's gun! I found it at his place the other day when I went looking for my mail."

"You mean you broke into Rafe's house?" my

mum said in exhausted disbelief. She inhaled and exhaled loudly.

"I had to! To get the drawings! He lied to you, Mum. The envelope *was* for me!"

"Cal . . ." my mum sighed.

"I found the gun in his drawer," I said, "and he came back for it when he was supposed to be out with you at the lawyer's! Where would I get a gun from, Mum? Think about it! You can't just walk into Kmart and buy one! And Rafe reckons he heard my voice? He's lying! I don't know why, but he's lying! And Gabbi must know that they're after me! She was probably just trying to scream out and warn me!"

"Well why did you run away when the police came? Oh, Cal, forget it. Please just come home. We can talk about it then. Darling, we know you wouldn't mean to hurt anyone. You can't even remember doing it."

"*I didn't do it!* How could I remember something I never did?" I said, infuriated. "Who's feeding you this crap? Mum, it's me, Cal, your son! What's wrong with you?" She was convinced I was guilty – that I'd hurt Gabbi – that I'd shot my uncle!

"Please believe I don't blame you!" she said. "I *know* what you've been through – you've had the worst possible time of all of us. Please Cal, we can get help for you!"

"That's not the sort of help I need!" I shouted. This was impossible. I couldn't explain my innocence over the phone. "Mum, you've got to believe me!"

"Please, Cal. Just come home. You can't imagine what I'm going through! I feel like I'm losing both of my children!" Her voice broke and she started sobbing again.

"Mum," I said calmly. "I didn't do it. Please get that through your head. Once I've proved that I'm innocent I'll come home. Something so much bigger than you can ever imagine is going on —"

My phone beeped a warning: Battery Low. I'd need to swap the battery over with the spare one Boges gave me.

Suddenly a man's voice came on the line. "Callum? Is that you?"

"Who's that?" I asked.

Then I realized. The cops were there with my mum!

I hung up instantly.

19 JANUARY
347 days to go . . .

5:03 am

I'd had the nightmare yet again. The same terrifying images and feelings had disturbed my sleep: being lost and helpless, shivering with fear and cold. I woke up in a sweat, and filled with despair.

It was starting to get light and I got up and washed my face with cold water. How could a toy dog be terrifying? It didn't make sense. But the reality I was living was also a nightmare – Gabbi saying I was the one who hurt her, Rafe saying he heard me in the house, my prints all over the gun, my own mother not believing me . . . there was no escape.

23 JANUARY
343 days to go . . .

9:21 pm

Another week had passed and I was finding things really hard. Life in hiding seemed to get worse.

Every morning, I'd spread the drawings out on the floor and study them. These were my work, my focus. I made notes, and scribbled down any ideas that came to me. I knew that in some way, they were connected to me, to my family.

Most days I'd go outside the back door where the lopsided tin roof– all that was left above the old porch – sheltered me, and there I'd have something to eat from the supplies Boges had given me.

Then I'd go back to the drawings . . .

Time passed so slowly. Under the cover of darkness, I slipped out to buy more food, and batteries for my flashlight.

25 JANUARY
341 days to go . . .

8:56 pm

I'd struggled to sleep the last couple of nights and was really feeling it.

I decided to copy the drawings for myself. I wanted to learn them, from the inside, hoping that they would reveal their secret to me. But what could I use as paper?

9:32 pm

I pulled a black marker out of my bag and stood by one of the walls. I looked down at the commando angel carefully and began copying his image directly onto the wallpaper. His form began to take shape as I bent low and stretched high to capture the size of his intimidating stature. Soon he towered above me.

I moved further along the wall and drew the monkey next, with his ball in hand, then the waiter carrying the tray of cards, the Roman emperor and the Sphinx, the cupboard and the number five, then the rose and the boy . . . I looked around at my surroundings and there was no answer. The images that I'd stared at nonstop since I found them at the mausoleum all glared at me from the walls, as if begging for my help. *I don't know!* I glared back.

Help me, Dad! I whispered in my head. *What were you trying to say when you drew these?*

I felt hopeless and pathetic. In frustration I began pulling off the wallpaper I'd just drawn on, tearing the giant angel down, ripping off his wings, tearing down the monkey and the Sphinx . . .

I fell to my knees and looked up at the mess I'd made. The image of the waiter was all that remained on the wall. He stared down at me, between half torn-off sheets of paper, and held out his tray. He offered me the jack and the ace of hearts. 21. 21! His two cards made a perfect 21 combination. A blackjack!

28 JANUARY

338 days to go . . .

Joe's Cafe
Macquarie Hills

12:24 pm
___

Why did the waiter have the winning combination on his tray? I needed help from Boges.

Being alone for so long in that decrepit old house was driving me crazy. The days were all blurring into each other. The drawings hadn't revealed anything else and I was no closer to finding out who had attacked my family and why. It had been too dangerous for Boges to meet with me and so he was trying to keep away until the heat died down. Time was ticking, and I was getting nowhere.

Back at the house I'd heard rats scampering around upstairs and thought I could smell something dead up there. The hot weather was making it worse.

I had to get out, so I'd taken the risk of sneaking out again in daylight.

I ordered something to eat in a small sandwich shop in a factory area. I sat at the table staring at the television, enjoying the first decent meal I'd had for a long time. Nobody paid any attention to me, until I nearly fell off my stool. I pretended it was because I had almost dropped my bag, but it was because my mother's face had suddenly filled the screen of the small TV set that sat on the shelf behind the counter.

"Please call me again, Cal," she pleaded. "We can sort this out. You must be ill. I don't blame you, and your uncle doesn't blame you either. We beg you to come home and help sort this out. There are good doctors who can help you deal with this." The camera panned back and there was Uncle Rafe, head bandaged, and arm in a sling, standing beside my mother as she spoke, a steadying hand on her shoulder.

I was speechless.

Mum, I wanted to say, *why don't you believe me? What's wrong with you?* Surely she knew her own son?

My mother spoke again. "We understand you've been under tremendous pressure lately. Just come home so we can deal with this together." She started crying and Rafe put his arm around her, pulling her close.

I wanted to call again, but I knew it was pointless.

My face flashed up on the screen again. But this time I didn't run or duck for cover – I didn't need to. I didn't look a thing like the fresh-faced schoolboy on TV anymore. He was history.

29 JANUARY

337 days to go . . .

Hideout
38 St Johns Street

10:29 am

My phone rang. Boges!

"They've stopped watching me. I think I can risk meeting you. What do you need?"

"More clothes," I said, "and more food."

Having such a good friend meant a lot to me, and without his help I didn't know what I would have done.

Soon all of my friends would be going back to school. I wondered what they thought of all this. Surely they didn't believe the reports.

They'd all soon be doing those ordinary daily things that had been part of my life for the last ten years, while I was forced to live like a criminal – on the run.

11:45 am

When Boges arrived at the derelict house, he stared at me, pointing to the studs in my lip and eyebrow and the tattoos on my neck and arms. "What happened to you?" he asked.

I touched my piercings and glanced at the tats. "They're fake," I said. "I had to make a few changes. I know it's lame, but it's a quick fix for now."

"You look gross!"

"And you've packed on a lot of weight suddenly!" I said, noticing how bulky he was looking.

"Thanks!" Boges shook his head and laughed. "I didn't want to carry a bag or anything, apart from this," Boges said, holding up a plastic bag of stuff he'd brought for me. "So I wore a few extra layers of clothes. Now I can peel them off and give them to you."

That's my friend Boges.

12:05 pm

Again, we were staring at the drawings spread out on the floor.

"See?" I pointed out the 21 to Boges.

"Yes, it's the winning combination," said

Boges. "A blackjack."

We stared at each other.

I looked more closely at my friend. "Are you OK?" I asked. "You look really white."

"It's just the heat," said Boges . . . "What happened in here?" he asked, looking around at the shredded wallpaper.

"Just a bit of interior decorating."

3:29 pm

We'd been poring over the drawings for hours, trying to make some sense out of the blackjack drawing. But so what? A blackjack. It could have just been a coincidence. My eyes ached and my brain felt wrung out like a wet sheet.

We were never going to crack these drawings — that is, if they could be cracked. After all, I reminded myself, my dad did have a virus that attacked his brain. Who knows what he was thinking.

The drawings that had seemed so intensely exciting a little while ago, that had seemed to mean something, now failed to interest me. The angel seemed like nothing but a long-dead image from a war that had been finished nearly one hundred years ago.

"We must be crazy to think these drawings

actually mean something."

'Come on, man," said Boges. "You're just feeling bad. Even the doctor said these drawings meant something to your father. What about your other relatives? Would they have helpful information about the family? Who else might know about the Ormond Riddle?"

"I don't have that many other relatives – except for a really ancient great-uncle who lives somewhere in the country. And some old great-aunt that I've never even met." I only had distant memories of my great-uncle, the uncle whose love of flying had been inherited by my dad. Dad had described him as a real character.

I started rubbing my shoulder. "I hurt it ages ago, somehow, but it's still aching."

Boges took a look. "It's a bit swollen."

"It won't kill me."

"But staying here might," said Boges. "You need a country holiday. And an ancient great-uncle is exactly the sort of guy who'd know a lot about the family. He's been around for a long time."

I must have looked unwilling because Boges kept talking, trying to convince me. It didn't work. "I don't know where he lives," I said.

"Tell me where I can find his address," said

Boges, "and I'll get it for you tonight."

I described a little book Mum kept near the telephone on the kitchen counter. I was pretty sure it would be in there.

9:40 pm

Later that night, as I sat outside on the back porch, wondering how I was going to get to the country, I was interrupted by a text message from Boges.

🗎 been throwing up for hours. so sorry. sick as. might be better in a couple of hours.

I couldn't wait. I would have to break into my own house.

30 JANUARY

336 days to go . . .

Home
Flood Street, Richmond

1:13 am

Huddled in the jacket that Boges gave me, I made my way home through the night. I moved quickly and quietly, constantly looking around for watchful eyes.

By the time I got to my street and peered around the corner, I was as jumpy as anything. Out of the dark, headlights suddenly blinded me as a car pulled out and headed my way. I dove sideways into the nearest garden, and crouched down until it passed. It was probably completely innocent – but I couldn't help suspecting everyone and everything.

I crept towards my house and was relieved to see that the only car there was my mum's.

As I came closer, I was shocked to find a "For Lease" sign standing in the front yard. Mum must have put the house up for rent. But where would she and Gabbi live? My heart sank. I could only guess where they would go: Rafe's house. The thought of that made me sick.

I crept around to the backyard and luckily the spare key was still under the cactus pot.

Moving like a ghost, I let myself in. Everything was quiet and dark.

I had to go through the living room to get into the kitchen, and once there I felt my way around until I found the little book beside the phone. Holding it up in the dim moonlight, I flipped through the pages until I found Great-uncle Bartholomew's address. I pulled a scrap of paper out of the trash and copied it down.

'Kilkenny'
Mount Helicon Road
Mount Helicon

A low growling noise came from behind me.
Shocked, I spun around.

Did Mum have a dog now, a guard dog?

I stood immobilized. But then my eyes adjusted
even more to the darkness . . .

1:20 am

There in front of me, lying along the sofa and
snoring loudly, was Uncle Rafe. He'd been hidden
by the back of the sofa when I came inside. If he
opened his eyes now, he'd be looking straight at
me!

I edged my way out of the kitchen, hardly
daring to breathe, gliding silently past the
sleeping figure, without taking my eyes off him.

I heard another noise behind me then, and
turned to see the figure of my mother coming
down the stairs.

I stepped backwards silently, taking cover
around the corner behind a tall bookcase. I held
my breath, terrified that she would hear me. She
came down into the living room, past Rafe and
then stopped, distracted by something on the
mantelpiece. She picked up a framed photograph
of Gabbi and me taken at the beginning of last
year, before Dad went to Ireland. Mum stared at
it for a long time. I noticed that in her other

hand she was holding the photograph of my father that she kept beside her bed.

I had to stand, silent and hidden, watching my mother's pain and grief. Both Mum and I had lost almost everything and I couldn't even comfort her.

I felt my own eyes sting with tears.

After awhile she turned and went back upstairs, holding the photographs close to her heart.

If only I could go back upstairs too, and crawl into my own bed. Maybe I should just turn myself in and get it over with, I thought. Then my eyes fell on the portrait of my parents on the wall, the shot taken when they'd taken a holiday together a few years ago. Even in the dim light it seemed that Dad's dark eyes were looking directly into mine, reminding me that I'd promised myself to take care of the family, that I'd promised myself to solve the mystery of the drawings and the Ormond Riddle. Standing in the dark, then and there, I made another promise to myself—that one day I'd walk back into this house, no matter who was renting it, pay them off and give it back to Mum. Then everything would be the way it once was. No, it would be better — way better than it had ever been. It would be as if Dad was back with us, because now I was more determined than ever to discover the huge secret he'd been in the process of uncovering. Whatever it might bring to us, it would always remind us of his presence.

As I made the promise, I felt a new strength and determination in my bones. Even though the situation right now seemed hopeless, if there was a way to do this, I was going to do it.

Hideout
38 St Johns Street

10:14 am

I was awake and eating more cold baked beans. I had made myself some big promises that I needed to keep. I had my great-uncle's address and I had to get ready to hit the road. All I needed was a map and a ride. But first, I had to see Boges.

I was packing my backpack with some supplies for the trip when Boges sent me a text.

📱 feeling heaps better 2day. but being watched. how did it go with the address? meet tomorrow @ 2 where we used to draw with chalk. bring them with you.

Straight away I knew where Boges meant, and what he wanted me to bring. In Year 8 we used to go to a five-story parking garage and hang out, writing stupid things on the walls.

The road trip would have to wait one more day.

📱 got the address. cool. see you there.

31 JANUARY

335 days to go . . .

Parking Garage
Liberty Mall

2:03 pm

I got there before Boges and went to the top level to keep a lookout for him.

It didn't take me long to spot him jogging along, and I was about to go down and meet him when I noticed a man following him. When Boges crossed the road, so did the man.

That's when I realized Boges was right. He *was* being followed and he was leading his pursuer straight to me!

I called him urgently. I watched as he pulled out his phone.

"Don't turn around! You're still being followed!" I told him. "Shake him off!"

Boges paused while he took the call, and so did the guy behind him. I could see him pretending to look at something on the ground.

Then Boges suddenly doubled back the way he'd come, almost colliding with the man as he straightened up. I ducked back from my lookout position.

2:19 pm

I heard something – it was Boges, huffing and puffing. "I took him on a wild goose chase," said Boges with a smile. "If you think I'm puffing, you should see him! We've been up and down and around and around! I sent him up and down in the elevator!" He plopped himself down on the ground, wiping his face. "Man, I'm glad that's over."

"Who do you think he was?" I asked.

"I reckon he was a cop. Out of condition. Too slow and heavy. I'm going to have to be very careful whenever we meet. This isn't the first time I've been followed."

"You're right. Boges, how's Mum?"

"So-so. Your uncle's out of the hospital."

"I know," I said. "He scared me to death last night. He was sleeping on the couch while I was breaking in."

"So you know about the plan to lease the house?"

I nodded.

"And Gabbi? How's she?"

"No change. She's still in a coma."

"But it's been nearly a month!" I said. "She's got to come around soon."

Boges looked away a moment and when he turned in my direction again, his face was very serious. "Cal, you should know that the doctors are saying she might never wake up."

"What?" I didn't want to hear what Boges was saying.

"With the sort of injuries she had," Boges continued, "and the fact that she was without oxygen for so long . . ."

I thought of my desperate attempts at CPR.

"She might have to be on life support for the rest of her life," said Boges.

I couldn't believe it. My heart flipped. I felt so helpless. I had to change the subject. "I'm heading off for the country," I said. "What did you want to tell me?"

"I've had an idea. About the drawings – the things that can be worn. That angel is wearing a lot of equipment. And some sort of medal."

I pulled out the drawing of the angel and we both looked at the medal just to the side of the gas mask.

"And you told me something was stolen from

your mum — some piece of jewelry? Again, something you *wear* . . ." he continued.

"Maybe," I said, "it was probably a gift for Mum — I'm just guessing it was jewelry. Mum said she'd never seen that box in her life."

I thought of something. "Maybe whatever was in that box was the Ormond Singularity. Some precious jewel or something? Something people will kill to get their hands on?"

"Error of logic, man," said Boges. "They've gotten their hands on it already. They're still trying to . . ."

". . . kill me," I finished for him. He was right. It had to be much bigger than a jewel.

"Look, Cal. I don't want to sound dramatic — you know I like to keep it simple, but I just want you to know that if anything were to ever happen to you, I'd follow this thing through for you."

A sudden sound near the stairwell brought the conversation to an end. A couple of security guards were hurrying towards us. "Hey, you two! What are you doing here?"

"Nothing," said Boges as we quickly rolled up the drawings. I shoved them deep into the back pocket of my bag.

"So go and do nothing somewhere else," the

ugliest security guard ordered. Then he looked past Boges at some graffiti on the wall. "Have you been vandalizing the walls?" he demanded. "What have you just put in that backpack? Come on, give it to me!"

That did it. Boges and I fled, racing down the ramps so fast that I thought we'd both hurtle straight out onto the road with such force that we'd be unable to stop, and get run over by a bus.

That didn't happen — we just yelled a hasty goodbye and split, Boges disappearing around the corner homewards, me heading back for my last night in the derelict house — I hoped. This city was getting too hot for me. Time I got out.

When I thought I'd thrown the security guards off the track, I slowed down, catching my breath. Boges was the best friend a guy could have, but he couldn't be with me on the run. He was still part of the normal world, and I wanted to keep it that way.

10:05 pm

I knew a couple of the bouncers outside the clubs by now, from my late night wanderings, and they sometimes shared a joke with me. So I sat hunched over a bag of chips that the guy in the takeout place gave me – in exchange for crushing all his cartons flat and stacking them in his trash cans in the back alley. He asked a few questions, but stopped when he saw me getting uneasy about the whereabouts of my family.

I decided to move on.

It wasn't far off midnight now. Tomorrow would be the beginning of February. That meant I'd been on the run for almost a month . . .

It also meant I'd survived the first month.

10:32 pm

With my head down, I hurried back towards the derelict house, crossing the shopping center where only a few people were scattered, heading homewards. I saw a group of guys at the far end who seemed to be involved in an argument outside the casino, and I was crossing the road to avoid them when I realized that there were three men pounding on one guy, who lay curled up helpless on the pavement.

Instinctively, I started yelling, "Hey! Stop!"

They ignored me.

"Police!" I yelled out, louder.

This time the three attackers stopped what they were doing, looked around, then started running, leaving their victim slowly crawling away. I hurried over to him, trying to help him to his feet, but ended up propping him up against a wall instead. As I did, he made a feeble attempt to escape, pushing me away, muttering, "Police, I gotta get away!"

"It's OK," I said. "There aren't any police coming. I just said that to get those guys away from you."

Now that the danger had passed, I took a closer look at the guy I'd helped. He was about twenty, I guessed, and had a black shirt, a silver chain around his neck, and a purple teardrop tattoo under his left eye. He pulled his legs close up to his body and was moaning. Blood dripped from his nose.

"Do you want a doctor?" I asked. I'd seen a medical center not far from the backpacker hostel. "Do you think you're hurt bad?"

"You mean there are no cops? You were just saying that? Why?" he spoke slowly, revealing bloody teeth. For some reason, I felt he was familiar, but I quickly put the thought out of my mind.

"Just to get those guys off you," I explained.

But now, in the distance, I *could* hear a siren wailing. Maybe someone else had called the police. And now that sound meant trouble for me. It was time to go back to my lair.

Slowly, the man came up real close to my face. "You mean, you just wanted to stop me getting beaten up?"

"You got a problem with that?" I asked. In the silence that followed, I started to feel uneasy.

The sound of the siren was coming closer. It was time to get out.

The man with the teardrop tattoo offered me his grazed hand.

"They think I'm working on the sly with the casino, to cheat them in poker. You've saved me from getting bashed to death."

Hesitatingly, I shook his hand.

"The name's Kelvin."

I'd heard that name just a while back. Now here was another one. I grabbed a name out of the air. "Tom," I said, thinking of my dad's name. "Hope you're all right, but I gotta go."

As Kelvin scrambled to his feet, I heard the sound of glass smashing behind me. Instinctively, I turned. One of Kelvin's attackers had returned and although he was already running away again, jumping into a waiting car, it was obvious he'd thrown something through the now gaping front window of the casino.

As the car took off, I was rocked by a deafening explosion, followed by the roar of flames. In seconds, the front of the building was engulfed in fire. The casino had been fire-bombed! What if there were people inside? I couldn't just run away and leave them. I ran towards the fire, thinking I might be able to help put it out. But I soon stopped. The flames roared impossibly high into the night sky, sending up angry sparks.

I stumbled backwards a few steps, driven away by the heat. Another explosion and the entire building was blazing.

Transfixed, I stood watching. Then I heard the sirens again.

Time for me to disappear.

11:02 pm

I made a fatal error.

I stopped being vigilant.

I was so fixed on the fire that I failed to notice the car that had pulled up behind me, until it was too late.

"Hey! What are you doing?" I yelled as the black Subaru skidded right up to me. The back door swung open and I was dragged inside. "*Let me go!*"

"Shut up and stop struggling and you won't get hurt!"

This was becoming a habit and I didn't like it. I struggled as hard as I could, but my kicking legs were pinned down and my arms were wrenched behind me.

"We can do this the hard way or the easy way," said my captor, a solid guy wearing a red tank top with a black Chinese symbol on it. "Keep still and I'll let go of your arms."

"OK, OK!" I said. "Who are you? What do you want?"

"You look real different from your picture in the papers," said Red Tank Top. "But we know who you are."

"Hey!" I yelled again. "What do you think you're doing?" He'd grabbed my backpack and was pulling my gear out, looking through it.

Was he after the drawings too?

That's when I saw the driver of the car. He was the same heavily built guy who'd followed Boges. He hadn't been a cop after all.

"Who are you?" I repeated. "And what do you want?"

"The boss wants a little chat with you, sonny."

Who were these people? Did they work for the woman who'd interrogated me earlier? Was she the woman who'd called me? If that woman got me again, I was in big trouble. I felt a chill spread from the base of my spine.

UnKnown Location

11:26 pm

I tried to see where the car was going, but I was held down on the back seat. Finally, we stopped and I managed to sit up a bit. It looked like we'd reached some sort of industrial area with a parking lot. The driver was waiting for the big gates to open. Once they were wide enough, the car drove through and parked.

"Where are we going?" I asked.

I was pulled out of the car and hauled up some steps into a room — what looked like an office with a large desk and a couple of chairs.

I could feel fear spreading through my body. Last time I'd been dragged off the street, I'd ended up listening to people suggesting I should be thrown off a cliff. I was terrified about what might happen this time.

I looked around the office and through the door came a very rotund guy in a dark suit, wearing a red spotted cravat pinned with a huge diamond. His thin hair was brushed back from a blotchy, sweaty forehead and his lower features were crowded together as if they were all trying to push out of his pouchy face.

"Who are you?" I yelled, attempting to sound brave. "And why have you dragged me here?"

Behind him a girl walked into the office and even though I was shaking with fear and dread, I couldn't take my eyes off her. She had wild dark hair with strips of ribbon and glittering threads tangled in it like webs, and the strangest eye makeup I have ever seen – green and gold stripes, like the rising sun, fanned out from her eyelids. Her green and gold skirt swirled around her when she moved, and her cool, gray eyes held mine. There was something mesmerizing about her . . .

I was shoved roughly into a chair and two wide strips of strong packing tape were strapped down on my wrists, tying me down. There was no point in struggling, but my heart was thumping in terror.

"I've already told you everything I know," I said, "when you had me last time. When that woman was questioning me."

"Woman? What woman? What did she look like?" asked the man with the pouchy face.

"Red hair. Purple sunglasses," I answered

automatically. But what was I saying? I'd never even *seen* her!

To my shock, the man with the pouchy face turned to Red Tank Top. "*She* must have gotten to him already! I told you we had to act fast! She was at the conference. They might be further ahead than we are!"

They knew her?! It was very clear now that two criminal groups were after the information about the Ormond Singularity.

Pouchy Face swung around at me again. "So, Callum Ormond, what did you tell her?"

"Who are you?" I asked.

"What did you tell her?" he repeated slowly and angrily. "And how do you know her?"

"I don't know her! I thought you did!"

Pouchy Face turned a deep purple-red. Without warning, he spat on the floor, then ground his heel into the wet spot. "Know her! That's what I think of her! You want to know who I am? Who wants to tell him?" he bellowed, challenging the others.

"No!" I yelled. "I don't wanna know! Just let me go! I won't tell anyone what's happened!"

"He won't tell anyone," sneered Red Tank Top to Pouchy Face. Then he turned to me. "You're not thinking of going to the cops, are you?"

"The man's name is Vulkan Sligo," said another voice from behind me, "and he is *the man*."

Vulkan Sligo? His name was familiar. I'd seen it in the press and on the news from time to time. Vulkan Sligo, nicknamed "the Slug," was a criminal whose name was sometimes mentioned in connection with a really famous crime boss, Murray "Toe Cutter" Durham. My dad had done a documentary on him a couple of years back. You never forget a name like Sligo's.

I swung my head around to see who was speaking and saw another heavily-built bodyguard in a suit jacket and black turtleneck coming up behind me.

The warnings in my father's letters filled my mind. I knew now that I was in massive danger. Not only was I on the run from the authorities, but I'd gotten myself into a position between *two* separate criminal groups – I was the meat in the sandwich.

Two! And both groups were onto my dad's secret, and both were trying to extract the same information from me. First the woman and her gang, and now Vulkan Sligo's mob.

"We know your father wrote to you from Ireland. So don't bother denying it. What did he tell you about the angel?"

The angel, I thought. Everybody wants to know about the angel. Including me! But I was determined not to give these people anything. I gave him a defiant look, even though my voice was shaky when I spoke.

"He didn't tell me anything about any angel." That at least was partly true.

"We heard from the hospice that your father did some drawings that were sent to you."

How did they know that? Then I thought of the woman who'd called me – Jennifer Smith. I ignored him.

"OK, let's try something else. Do you know anything about a jewel? What about the Ormond Riddle?"

"Nothing! The only reason I've even heard about these things is because people I don't know – first that woman – and now you – keep grabbing me and asking me about them! Just let me go!"

I was angry now. My arms were getting cut up from the packing tape. "If I knew anything about some stinking angel, jewel or riddle I'd be happy to tell you. But I don't know anything. Just let me go!" Somehow, I'd kept my voice strong and steady.

It was no use. The questions went on and on, always the same, and my answers went on and on, always the same.

Red Tank Top slapped me hard across the face. "You'd better tell us what we want to know."

Or else what? I thought.

"Go and take the cover off the tank!" said Sligo, gesturing outside with his head. At that moment Red Tank Top kicked me and my chair towards the window. He grabbed my head roughly and shoved it around so that I was looking down into the parking lot. Then he left the office area and went outside. An automatic light came on below. Red Tank Top walked into view, bent over and removed what looked like a manhole cover. The hole, like a pitch black circle in the ground, revealed an opening to an underground area.

"That's our sump oil storage tank," explained Sligo, with a very unpleasant smile on his face. "See that tanker over there? It's due to be pumped out, any minute now."

Just beyond the lit area, but parked close enough for me to see it, was a huge long-haul tanker. I didn't want to know why Sligo was telling me all this.

Meanwhile, Red Tank Top had returned. He spun me around again on the chair so that Sligo could push his face right into mine. "Listen, kid," Sligo snarled, "you tell me everything right this minute."

I was truly terrified now.

"You tell me what I want to know or I am going to throw you down into that empty storage tank and screw the manhole cover down real tight. Then we'll pump in the tanker's load, and fill it right up to the top. No one will ever find you down there. But don't worry, you'll die quickly."

"But you've got to believe me!" I said, my voice shaking, my whole body trembling. "If I knew anything, I'd tell you! I swear!"

"That's enough," said Sligo. "I'm done with this boy. Take him down." Red Tank Top wrenched off the tape that was strapping my arms to the chair.

"No! Please! I don't want to die! I don't know anything. I'd tell you if I did!"

I could feel the sweat dripping off me. I looked around for the girl with the strange eyes – surely she couldn't stand by and let this happen to me. But she was nowhere to be seen.

Red Tank Top tore the final strip of tape off

and hauled me out of the chair, with a bruising grip. Sligo started to walk out the door, throwing my backpack in the trash.

"*Please!*" I begged, "I swear I know *nothing* about the angel – all I know is that there are drawings!"

Sligo paused by the door, then turned.

"Get rid of him."

11:50 pm

Kicking and screaming furiously, I was dragged out of the office and down the stairs.

Red Tank Top hauled me over to the gaping black hole of the underground storage tank.

"No!" I yelled. But he was too strong for me. Despite my desperate struggles, he pushed me down and I half fell into the circular opening, bashing my shins painfully on the rungs of a steel ladder. I tried scrambling back up out of the hole, but Red Tank Top kicked me hard then forced me back down the ladder, pulling the manhole cover into position, almost taking my fingers off as he did.

It was pitch black down there and I clung to the steel ladder, frantically trying to think of a way to escape. Once they'd gone, maybe I'd be able to open the lid and get out. I pushed it, but it was firmly locked into place.

Blindly, I felt my way around the walls. It stank of oil. My feet were slipping on the ground, and I kept struggling to get back up again. The tank was about the size of a small bathroom, and if I stood on my toes I could touch the roof.

There was no way out.

The sudden scraping of metal made me hope for a minute that my kidnappers had changed their minds and were letting me out. But what I saw filled me with unimaginable horror.

A small cover had been removed and now a steel pipe dangled through it. Within a few seconds, the pipe started spurting thick sump oil. They were filling the tank! With me inside! If I didn't get out fast, I would drown.

Already, the oil was covering my shoes. I felt my way back to the steel ladder, clawing my way up. I banged my head on the manhole cover. I bashed on it, yelling, "Let me out! *Let me out! You can't do this!*"

The stinking oil kept spurting in, gurgling into the tank. I crouched on the highest level of the ladder that I could fit on, pushing the manhole lid as hard as I could with my back and shoulders. It wouldn't budge.

Squashed up on the topmost level, I begged for the oil to stop pouring in. But it didn't. I could feel the stinking, viscous mess covering my feet, then my shins and my knees.

I lashed out against the cover, with the full force of my whole body, but there was nothing I could do.

Now the oil had climbed my legs and was at my waist. I had to raise my hands to avoid its thick, suffocating clamminess.

The oil relentlessly poured in. I could feel it slowly creeping up my chest. I could hardly move my legs or arms through its thickness. The stench was stifling.

This was it. I would never see my family again.

I closed my eyes and thought of Gabbi, lifeless in the hospital. I prayed that she'd make it. I thought of my poor mum, so alone and so completely confused. I thought of my dad. He'd saved me from drowning before, but I knew he couldn't help me now. He'd had such faith in me, and I'd failed him . . . Lastly, I thought of Boges, my friend, and hoped he'd keep his promise to me.

I took a deep breath and closed my mouth as the oil reached my chin. It quickly climbed my face. I spat the stinking oil from my lips and strained desperately to move higher. My head was already hard against the ceiling of the tank, there was nowhere else to go. Any minute now, the oil would completely cover my mouth, then my nose . . . and then I'd be gone.

AS RACE AGAINST TIME 06:48 07:12 05:21 RACE AGA
ICE AGAINST TIME SEEK THE TRUTH... CONSPIRACY
E SOMETHING IS SERIOUSLY MESSED UP HERE 08:3
06 06:07 JUNE WHO CAN CAL TRUST? SEEK THE TI
NE 06:04 10:08 RACE AGAINST TIME 02:27 08:06 10
E TRUTH 01:00 07:57 SOMETHING IS SERIOUSLY ME
01 09:53 CONSPIRACY 365 12:00 RACE AGAINST TIM
NE WHO CAN CAL TRUST? 01:09 LET THE COUNTDOW
NE HIDING SOMETHING? 03:32 01:47 05:03 JUNE LE
UNTDOWN BEGIN 09:06 10:33 11:45 RACE AGAINST TI
12 05:21 RACE AGAINST TIME RACE AGAINST TIME S
UTH... CONSPIRACY 365 TRUST NO ONE 06:07 SOM
RIOUSLY MESSED UP HERE 08:30 12:01 05:07 06:06
HO CAN CAL TRUST? SEEK THE TRUTH 12:05 JUNE 06
ICE AGAINST TIME 02:27 08:06 10:32 SEEK THE TRUT
57 SOMETHING IS SERIOUSLY MESSED UP HERE 05:0
NSPIRACY 365 12:00 RACE AGAINST TIME 04:31 10:17
N CAL TRUST? 01:09 LET THE COUNTDOWN BEGIN JU
METHING? 03:32 01:47 05:03 JUNE LET THE COUNTI
06 10:33 11:45 RACE AGAINST TIME 06:48 07:12 05:2
AINST TIME RACE AGAINST TIME SEEK THE TRUTH...
S TRUST NO ONE SOMETHING IS 06:07 SERIOUSLY M
RE 08:30 12:01 05:07 06:06 06:07 JUNE WHO CAN CA
EK THE TRUTH 12:05 JUNE 06:04 10:08 RACE AGAINS
06 10:32 SEEK THE TRUTH 01:00 07:57 SOMETHING
ESSED UP HERE 05:01 09:53 CONSPIRACY 365 12:00
ME 04:31 10:17 JUNE WHO CAN CAL TRUST? 01:09 LET
UNTDOWN BEGIN JUNE HIDING SOMETHING? 03:32 0
NE LET THE COUNTDOWN BEGIN 09:06 10:33 11:45 R
ME 06:48 07:12 05:21 RACE AGAINST TIME RACE AGA
EK THE TRUTH... CONSPIRACY 365 TRUST NO ONE S
07 SERIOUSLY MESSED UP HERE 08:30 12:01 05:07
NE WHO CAN CAL TRUST? SEEK THE TRUTH 12:05 JU
08 RACE AGAINST TIME 02:27 08:06 10:32 SEEK THE
57 SOMETHING IS SERIOUSLY MESSED UP HERE 05: